Phoenix in me

Selena Đorđević-Marquardt

Phoenix in me by Selena Đorđević-Marquardt
Published 2024 by Your Book Angel
Copyright © 2024 Selena Đorđević-Marquardt

Printed in the United States
Edited by Keidi Keating
Layout by Rochelle Mensidor

ISBN: 979-8-9897121-8-2

TO ALL THE BIG DREAMERS

"I no longer feared the darkness once I knew the phoenix in me would rise from the ashes."

William C. Hannan

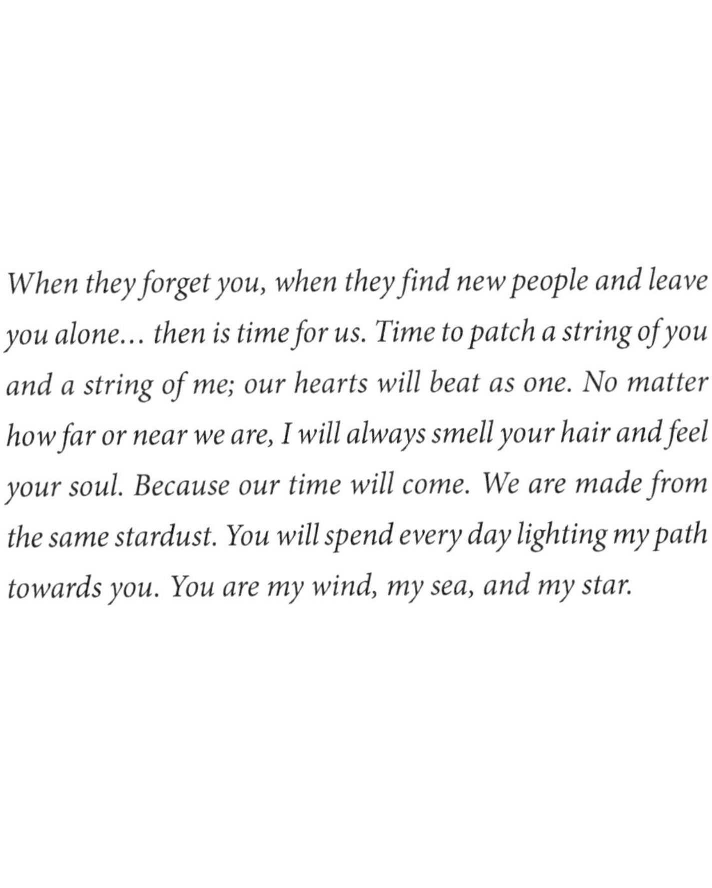

When they forget you, when they find new people and leave you alone… then is time for us. Time to patch a string of you and a string of me; our hearts will beat as one. No matter how far or near we are, I will always smell your hair and feel your soul. Because our time will come. We are made from the same stardust. You will spend every day lighting my path towards you. You are my wind, my sea, and my star.

Prologue

And I whispered: 'Forget the past. Remember that might be no future. There is only here and now. You and me. And science. And God.'

(2019.)

My hands are soaked in blood. I am holding the knife; my whole body is numb. I am shaking, sitting in his blood. Blood-soaked daisies are around me. I am looking at the lifeless body. My mind can't think and my heart is beating too slow. *He's dead.* That's all that I ponder and feel. No tears, no sounds. Except for when I call the police. I lean and kiss his lips one more time. I am surprised that they are still warm. I look into his eyes but there is no life in them anymore. No emotions. *He's gone.* I close his eyelids.

When the police enter the flat, naturally they cuff me and bring me to the station. In all fairness, I was holding the knife, covered in blood. They are asking questions, but even if I hear them, there is no voice left in me to reply.

I look at them and the only thing that could come out is, "He is dead." The police call a lawyer for me, and I make a phone call to Sophie. "I am at the police station. Call my mother and ask for help. He's dead." Then I hang up.

I don't know how much time I am spending in the station. There is more blood that needs to be collected from my body as evidence. I smoke lots of cigarettes. I cry silent tears. Sophie is in shock, even I can feel that, but she is holding herself together.

"I called your mother. She is sending a lawyer; her and Luca will be on the first plane out. Everything will be fine."

Of course, I hate to hear the words–*everything will be fine*–in that moment, but what else should she say? At least Luca is coming, he'll bring me good medications, to sedate this whole existence of mine, until I wake up and realize that all of this was a dream.

Luca arrives at the police station, together with the lawyer, after about a day. Which was plenty of time for me to spend in a cell, with no one to bail me out, like *I* killed the love of my life. My mother is probably just waiting in a hotel room, drinking her martini, and thinking how I made another mistake. But Luca and the lawyer came and whatever happens next, I will not recall. I will be medicated and all will be a blur. At least for some days.

He is dead. And how could I continue living now?

* * *

(High school period, 2003.)

My name is Masha and I was born on a full Moon. It must be that my mother was waiting patiently until that day, so that she could somehow give me some superpowers of the Moon Goddess. She was always very posh and dramatic, so she wanted her girl to be special. It turned out that I was not Barbie-like, and I wouldn't win pageants. I am just a girl-next-door. Nothing special. Always on the run, dreaming, searching for love while working hard.

I am a first-generation American citizen. My mother is Greek, from a small island near Athens, called Aegina. My father is from the Belarusian capital, Minsk. And in my house, we don't need additional excitement and loudness from the outside. Actually, I think people come to our house to watch live tv shows with my parents being the main characters.

I hid in my room and imagined being at college, far from home, for most of my young years. Embarrassed by my parents yelling, without a brother or sister to share the suffering. My best friends were my stuffed animals. All of them were my patients that I practiced on for my school of medicine.

And I love to read. Reading is my passion. I read everything and anything. Romance and fairy-tales completely ruined me. I would imagine that I could be like Tatyana in Puskin's Onegin, and that someone will love me so strongly and passionately, with a happy ending, of course. *Oh, such a silly girl.* Honestly, someone should explain to girls that what they read or watch, is not that perfect or true.

(2015.)

Waiting for that package to come. Every day I am waiting for that package to come. Life became a collection of package arrivals, mixed with opening them and sorting the contents into different positions in the house. Life became that dopamine release before I click *buy*. And short endorphin boosts when I place the items on their shelfs. Someone would say, "oh wow, you are depressed!" Imagine, how did you come up with that? Sarcasm… Oh, yes, another thing that I love. But only when it is *not* directed towards me. My ego hurts like hell then. I'm proud that I can at least recognize that.

I love my ego. I love how it can boost me when no one else does. So, I cherish it and I click *buy*, because I know that my hormones keep me alive and my ego happy. Because, I do want to live. I am not an ungrateful bitch, that does not want to appreciate how life was given to us and we should do the best we can, every day. So, I do. I do my job, and I click *buy*.

I like to cheer to myself from time to time. For example, how I managed through another week. Or how I did not hit that arrogant lady in the supermarket. So, I say to myself: "Well done, Masha. You made it. You did the best you could do today."

I have a dog named Christoph, and he is my best friend. If I would be honest, forget the packages and my ego, I love Christoph the most. I got him from my ex-boyfriend, called Lucky in the circles. I guess Christoph was a pity present, for forgiving him for cheating on me. But that was the best thing that happened during the two years we were together. Yes, he flirted around and eventually cheated, but I got Christoph and those eyes gave me courage to end the relationship. So, thank you, Lucky. I appreciate that you at least had the taste to choose a wonderful puppy for me, even though I am sure you had no idea what you were doing. Or Lucky's brother helped, that would make much more sense. He was always the more sensible one of the two of them.

I was quite an intelligent kid. I loved books; I still do (you can see my Amazon shopping history). I try to take care of how many of them I buy since I don't have that much space in my apartment. And I really can't stand when books are laying on the floor; they look like some kind of decoration. I do not agree with that. *Nope.* Books deserve their own shelf and table.

So, I was an intelligent kid, who read lots of books and who wanted to get as many degrees as I could. Essentially, I became the first scientist in the family and even finished my PhD in Neurobiology. Total nerd.

However, this nerd somehow managed to get all the degrees with being a night owl. Maybe Christoph did some exams for me? I learned that I do have a wild side, one that wants to experience all that life can offer.

After my first boyfriend in the first year of college, I became a true heartbreaker. I was letting boys chase me, then making out with them and breaking their hearts by never answering their calls. I was choosing guys that were the least compatible with me. I was smoking a lot of cigarettes during my studies, also throughout my PhD. I was drinking and vomiting, sometimes people would just leave me in the ER, sometimes in front of my apartment door. Blackouts were frequent and not so pleasant. Those days I was convincing myself and my mother, even though she did not know the severity of the whole situation, that I had no hope for further studies and I just should be a bartender. Or one of those actresses that wait forever for a commercial while serving some "big" names in the business.

Was I happy at that time, that was the question my physiatrist asked me later on; no, not really. I was at best, carefree. I was not having the issue that my prefrontal cortex would overwork, and I would black out. Which was the case very often during my high school years. Doctors had different opinions: cancer *(of course),* epilepsy, some rare syndrome without a name…. Until I met one doctor who just said, "This kid needs a break. And a quiet home. That is why her brain shuts off and lets itself rest for a few seconds." That sounded pretty reasonable, until I grew up no one knew or thought that kids can have panic attacks and can deal with them in their own way, especially if the family situation wasn't so optimal.

My parents got divorced when I was twelve and my father was sending money to my mother for me mainly, but she was also taken care of.

I didn't have much contact with my father since he moved out. From time to time, I would talk with my half-sister, but that was so painful since she was so full of herself. I was happy not to have any contact with her when our father died. Which happened during my PhD studies. I saw my half-sister at the reading of the will. I have chosen Minneapolis, Minnesota, as the city where I would enroll for my PhD in Neurobiology. There I saw her the next time, in some of the pubs. She barely said hi, but I wasn't surprised, the world was always spinning around her. Some guys were asking me, "Hey, who is that girl?" I would say no one and just ignore the next request to get them introduced.

My father gave a fair share of his money to both families and for my mother that was important. He also left us the house at Bel Air, and my mother did not have to leave her everyday lifestyle. Doing nothing. Or playing tennis. We were set for life. And my college fund was big enough. But what would that matter if I didn't continue my studies?

* * *

I loved to observe the behaviour of animals. There is so much you can learn about humans by observing other mammal species. So I decided to do that, to observe different mammals and compare their social behaviour, trying to conclude how that impacts evolution of the human brain and to predict our future development. *Prediction* is not the most desired word to use in science. You should use something like *hypothesis*, or *assumption*, but my nerdy rebellion did not care about that. Throughout PhD, I was writing with my style, and somehow, my peers liked that. At least *that*, if not me in general. I was not their typical scientist type. Not how I behave, not how I dress, but I always told the truth, and I was always looking for the truth. And that they did like. So, I continued telling my truth. And nothing but the truth.

And here it goes. My personal truth.

My story that I want to tell started one day in Rome. One autumn Roman day… It also started one spring day, full of snow, in Minneapolis. My story has several beginnings, but only one ending.

100,000 Thoughts Per Day

"I know your window and I know it's late
I know your stairs and your doorway
I walk down your street and past your gate
I stand by the light of the four-way."

Downtown train by Tom Waits

When the whole world crushes on top of you, and you are young and full of life, you find yourself in a state of *now I must get up and become adult quickly.* But how can you be an adult that knows to manage life, if you have never had a true example of how mature people behave? I was going from one mistake to another, from one crisis to the next, all by myself. One parent dead, another interested more in the tennis court than what is happening in the real world.

It became hard to breath. I literally could not take a deep inhale. My brain was on fire. I was thinking more than what an average brain would think. My thoughts were scattered and mostly they were about fear. Fear of life, fear of tomorrow, fear of criticism, of never being good enough. What I understand now is that the fear and the insecurity that I started to feel during my years in Minnesota, were crucial for the years to come. All other pain that I later felt was due to low self-esteem, which sneaked into my life because I was not able to process and overcome the emotions from that period of my life. And from my childhood; there is always that past trauma that you do not even remember.

It was overwhelming. And it was enough. I was standing in the middle of my room, and I knew that Mauricio, my first big love, would come home from work to my place that day. Well, he was coming to my place more often that last month anyways. I did not know how to break up with him. Being with him was breaking my heart, but not being with him was unbearable, too. Something had to be done though. I was realizing that I really needed to take that deep breath soon…

* * *

I fell for Mauricio one spring day in Minnesota, during my PhD studies. He was tall, he looked a little bit like Keanu Reeves, and he was smart. *So smart.* I was hooked immediately. I did not know how I would be with him, how he would notice me. While I was listening to his speech during Neuroscience class, he was a Postdoctoral researcher brought by our professor to give a lecture in cognitive behaviour and brain function, my whole body was shivering. I was on fire without being sick. Our eyes met a few times, but that was a normal situation when you are in the audience of 30 people. Chances are pretty good. How to get him to talk to me, that was another story.

Instead of using my knowledge, approach him and ask some smart questions, I followed him with my friend and roommate, Maggie, to the next place where he would go. *I was literally stalking him.* He met a few guys in front of the building, they greeted each other like they haven't seen each other for a long time and started walking. Maggie and I really hoped that he would not turn to see us. And he didn't. The group entered a nearby bar. So, the next logical thing was that Maggie and I would have an early beer, while not having had any lunch. Because, why not?

We sat at the table across from the group and ordered our drinks. I was trying to make eye contact with Mauricio, but he was avoiding me so nicely, that it made me furious. Like he knew I was firing shots at him. It was frustrating. After a while, I decided to stop searching for the opportunity for him to pay any attention to me and start having fun with Maggie. We worked hard for our degrees and we were allowed to blow off some steam.

* * *

Maggie and I really enjoyed those first months at the University. We were studying together, partying together, living together. Our place was located close to the campus, and not living at home was such a blast. We ended up loving the bar where we once followed Mauricio to and started to spend a lot of time there. Sometimes the whole day. We would start early in the day with a coffee while writing our laboratory journals that we'd have to finish that day for the next meeting with our supervisor; and end the day with God knows how many beers. We met so many interesting people and enjoyed having fun.

When I think about Maggie, she was probably my best friend I ever had. She knew everything about me that could be known at the time. And she never judged.

She was fun, intelligent, loyal, but also honest and direct. She knew what she wanted and how to get it. She was the piece that I was missing, true free spirit overflowing with confidence. She made me feel good and safe. I could be myself beside her. Ending of our friendship was one of the hardest things that happened to me. I still don't know the reason why we stopped talking when we finished PhD, but it was just over. She showed that she is ready to move on from me. I wish I know what I did wrong. It was hard to take in. I never had, to this day, a friend like she was to me back then.

The whole drama that happened between Mauricio and me, happened in front of Maggie's eyes. She knew everything. Thinking back, maybe that was what broke our friendship. Maybe she could not look at me anymore, crying a lot and being hurt by someone like that. She might have reached the limit of seeing me in pain and doing nothing to avoid it.

* * *

With so much experiments to be done in the following weeks, I've almost forgotten about the tall, dark-haired guy that left me speechless and feverish with his way of speaking. *Almost.* Until I met him again in the same bar where Maggie and I followed him, after the lecture that he gave to my class.

This time, he did see me sitting across his table and he smiled at me. That one smile, *oh my God*, that was all it took for me to remember how I felt the first time I saw him, and to introduce me for the first time in my life to the feeling of being completely, madly, deeply, falling for some guy. That feeling was unfamiliar to me, I have not felt that for my first boyfriend. Lucky only ever made me feel giddy, until he wasn't, but I was never really in love. Crush and brief lust were all that I felt. Until Mauricio's look. One of the guys from Mauricio's table approached Maggie and me, and invited us to join their crew for drinks. Mauricio reached out to me with his hand and introduced himself. He was smiling all evening. There was something about him that screamed mystery, and at the same time misery. It was noticeable that he dressed nicely, and he was freshly shaved. His hair was pulled backwards with gel, making him look even more composed. His hands were soft, and his nails nicely trimmed. He talked about his research as a Postdoc at the Institute that was adjacent to the faculty of Biology, where he was part of the Neuroscience laboratory.

I considered myself to be a smart, strong girl, who knew what she wants. However, after that night, I became someone else, some version of me that I continued to be for the next couple of years. I became a silly, blind, naive little girl, trapped in my own fairy tale, and spellbound by the words of a very dangerous man. The man who would take your heart, squeeze it, and keep it squeezed until it bleeds out and crumbles into dust. Together with all your dreams and all your energy. I sold myself to the devil after the first kiss with Mauricio. The deal was signed. After the first time that we made love, I was already so deep into him that being separated even for a day was like coming off a drug. My whole body was in pain. I needed more of him. Every time after, I needed him a little more than the time before. I was losing my identity. I was studying for my degree, but it was more interesting to talk about science with him, then to go and actually do the research. Truth to be told, I was postponing finishing my studies, so that I'd have more time to talk to him about each subject, and being taught by him was all I needed. Yes, I was that deep into him.

* * *

Very organically he started to spend nights at my place, since I was closer to the good spots for nights out. Waking up next to Mauricio was such a good feeling. He was especially loving and gentle in the morning, after the alcohol wore off. And yes, he was drinking a lot. At the time, I didn't think that was a problem, we were going out with friends, we were all drinking. And we were having fun, all was fine, so I would remove any negative thoughts about that. Especially in the morning, when he would hug and kiss me and make love with me. That was another thing with Mauricio, with him I never felt that it is just sex. He was making me feel seen, wanted, desired. I was surrendering myself to him completely. In his eyes, I would see that he was present with me too. That he was falling in love with me, more and more with every time we were together. Once the alcohol wore off…

* * *

When one of Mauricio's friends realized how fast everything was developing between Mauricio and me, he approached me one day.

"Listen Masha, I don't want to see you hurt, you really are a nice girl." His voice was breaking.

"What is wrong, Jack? Are you okay?"

"No, no, I am fine. This is about Mauricio. So… I can see that the two of you are hanging out a lot, and that something more serious is happening. You, hm, look like you are really into him. And I think you should know…" He took a deep breath while I was looking at him, terrified by my own thoughts. *What is he going to say?* "Mao has a girlfriend. They've been together for like ten years already. She is the only constant in his life."

My heart felt like it got stabbed by hundreds of swords.

"What are you telling me, Jack? That is not true! I have never noticed anything. No calls, no texts while we are together. What the hell? That's not possible! He would not do that to me. I know he wouldn't!"

I started to have a panic attack. My first one, right then and there, in the middle of the bar, in front of Maggie and Jack. I was hyperventilating and cold sweat was going down my spine. Then I burst into tears.

"I am so sorry. But I really like you and I had to say something. Also, Mao doesn't know that you will be here in the bar today, right?" Jack continued to talk after I calmed down a bit.

"No, I told him that I would be with Maggie studying at home tonight, but we decided to come here, and thought it would be nice to surprise him." I replied, already scared about what Jack would say next.

"Well, yeah, he will be surprised for sure. He will be here any minute with his girlfriend."

I was frozen in a second. Maggie took my hand and said, "Maybe we should just go, Masha, what do you think?"

I took some deep breaths and finished my drink, *bottom's up.* "No, we stay. I want him to see me, and to know that I know."

Jack left the table, giving me a sad smile while going away. He was right, Mauricio and his girlfriend of apparently ten years, entered the bar some minutes later. She was tall, not very attractive, but she was his girlfriend. I felt so sad for her, for me, for both of us. When he saw me in the bar, his eyes filled with fear, and I guess he expected that I would explode and tell her that he has been cheating on her. But I had no plans to do that. I did not plan to make a scene in a bar where I am a regular guest and I know the owners. I just wanted him to see me knowing that he was a liar.

Before leaving the bar, I went to the restroom. Mauricio followed me there and locked the door behind him.

"Masha, I… I…"

"Yes, you lied. I see that."

"I am sorry. It's just hard. I've been with her for a very long time and then I met you, and I fell for you like never before. I have never done this. I mean, cheating… I… It is so confusing and frustrating."

"I am sorry too. My heart is literally breaking right now." I started to cry again.

He hugged me and I completely started to fall apart. I was sobbing in a smelly unisex restroom.

"It's so hard. *So hard.* I won't say anything except that I don't want to hear from you or see you. I am not the other woman."

And I exited the restroom. I grabbed my bag, told Jack to cover my bill, that I will come tomorrow to pay it, took Maggie's hand, and left the bar. I spent the whole night crying, rewinding past weeks and searching for red flags. How the hell did I not noticed anything?

* * *

A summer storm was raging outside. I could hear the roof of the house crying under the pressure of the heavy rain and branches. The lightening was intense. I was not used to this kind of storm as a kid from LA. This one was mimicking my soul in pain, and crying that did not stop for days. I could not focus on my studies after my break-up with Mauricio, so I called my mother and told her I was coming home for the summer. She was happy, I think. I was never sure what exactly she was feeling.

I missed her anyway. I missed my bed. My dolls and my books. I just wanted to crawl into my bed, cover myself with a blanket and sleep until I was so far in the future that I would barely remember the part of my life when I felt love.

Why do we love? *Why* do we deliberately choose to expose ourselves to the possibility that we can end up suffering? All the movies and the books show how love is beautiful. And yes, there were some troubles and obstacles to go over, but it was always a happy ending.

I shut my eyes, so that I didn't see the next flash of lightning coming and I made a wish to never be married or fall in love again. It hurts and it does not make any sense. It is far away from that joyous emotion that I was led to believe by every Hallmark movie.

* * *

Maggie was persistent with her messages and calls. She wanted to make sure that I'd wake up on time each day, eat and have regular walks. I was annoyed with her more than once.

"You are not my mother to control my steps! Not even she is doing that! I believe that she doesn't care how I am!"

"Exactly! That is why I am calling to check on you!" She yelled back at me. "Listen, I love you M, and you are strong. You need to tell yourself that every day! When is your father coming back from his business trip?"

"I believe today. He already postponed for a day. I miss him. He is the only one I can talk to." I was looking forward to seeing my dad, much more than seeing my mother. He understood me better than anyone. So, when he came that evening, after having dinner at his place, we sat in the garden and enjoyed the summer evening breeze. Now, that he was back, it had been already two weeks post-break-up and beside him I felt safe and secure. It was a bit easier to breathe. He sensed that something was happening in my life, more than just my excuse of needing a break from school this summer. He knew that I had big plans for my career, which he supported completely, so taking this break was a clear indication that I am in some kind of trouble.

"What is wrong, monkey?" He asked after some time observing the apple tree.

"All good, dad. Now all is good, you are back." I replied.

"Ahm. I guess that's the truth that I have to accept right now. Until you are ready to talk."

"I just… Did not expect adulting to be so hard. I mean… That people are… Sometimes… Not true to their words and actions."

"Is everything fine between you and Maggie?"

"Yes, we're fine." I replied and tried to hide the upcoming rivers of tears. But they were visible even in the evening light.

My dad took my hand and squeezed it.

"You know, monkey, you are right. Adulting is not easy. And I am glad that you are already seeing that. Better now than later. The sooner you know that people are not always who they say they are, the better. Trust is earned, not just given randomly. You're too good of a person and you tend to trust too easily. I guess now is the time to start working on that. Don't trust people until they show you, with actions, that they deserve your trust. And even then, a little bit of doubt is okay, for your own self-preservation. There will be many more guys in your life that will want your attention. You will be fine."

Of course, he knew it's about a guy. At that moment it felt like a stone lifted from my heart, and I started to cry like a baby. I just let all my emotions run through me. And my dad just continued to hold my hand while looking at the apple tree.

* * *

I was sitting in front of Mao's building and I cried and cried, not knowing why. My mother was trying to reach me on my mobile, but I was declining her calls. I was trying to reach *him*. Leaving desperate voice messages, ringing on the intercom, I wanted to see him so bad. His car was there, so he must have been in his apartment, it was past work hours.

The next call on my phone was from my uncle. That, I had to answer.

"Hello, Masha. Your mother was trying to reach you."

"I know, I am sorry. I'm just not feeling good, and not in such a mood of talking."

"Please go to your apartment and collect some necessary things, and catch the first flight to LA."

"Why uncle?" My voice was shaking. I felt in my uncle's voice that something is not right.

"Please, just do so and call your mother on the way."

I hung up. I somehow already knew what happened. Everything changed in a split second. That was the day when my father died.

∗ ∗ ∗

Since my father's funeral, Mao and me started to see each other again. This time, there was no girlfriend though. That is why I reconsidered. Something happened, and the two of them split after a decade of being together. Because of everything that was happening in my life, Mao left aside his story, and tried to be supportive of me as much as he knew how. But that was not enough. The pain of his breakup was too obvious.

Sometimes, Mao didn't reply to my messages for hours, days, or not at all. It was painful. He was my first love, I felt that I would never love again like I loved him. But he was using that to play with me, like a puppeteer. *Did he break up with his girlfriend because of me and now he is punishing me?* My brain didn't care. But my heart was suffering.

One day I felt that my heart was literally breaking. The doctors said that I had minor heart attack. My mother was freaking out, my friends were crying, and he… He was not there… He never visited me in the hospital. I hadn't even gotten a message. After a few days, I was out of the hospital, and the same evening he came to my flat.

"How are you?" He asked, standing at the door.

"Better."

My mother was sleeping at my place, since I did not want to be in my family home, and she wanted to stay close to me, to take care of me. Though, I'm not sure who was taking care of whom.

"My mother is here. If you want, you can come in."

"No, thank you. I just heard from your colleagues in the bar that you were in the hospital, so I wanted to check on you."

"Did you not have a cell phone to call? Or you were too busy to come to the hospital?"

I was angry for not hearing from him for days, and I really could not pretend that I liked him now. I loved him, but I didn't *like* him. Not tonight.

"I was busy."

"Fine. If you do not want to come in, I would like to go lie down. I am a bit tired. So, thank you for stopping by."

"Of course." He looked into my eyes, and I could see that he was worried. Then he turned and left.

I went to lie in bed. My mother asked me who it was. I said that it was my neighbour. Then I took a pill for sleeping that the doctor gave me and closed my eyes. There was no strength in me to think about anything. Tomorrow will come. New day. Fresh start.

* * *

"Your eyes have huge pupils. You are a drug addict! You are a pill addict!" He was yelling at me, while his eyes were red and threatening. I was crying and shaking, begging him not to yell anymore.

"I am leaving you; I am going now. You will never see me! You are a slut full of drugs!" He continued. Then he started to go towards the door.

I wanted to demand that he stays, that he apologizes for all those insults and lies, but I was just, through the waves of tears, saying, "Don't do this please, you will regret it. Don't yell. Don't go."

"You are a slut, police whore!" A long time ago, he heard that my family has some friends from a police department, and suddenly he remembered that fact and he was using it in every sentence.

I caught his arm. "Don't go. Please, stay. You do not know what you are saying."

"Who are you? What is your worth? You will never see me again."

"Stay please. You're drunk, and you will get hurt. Stay, sleep through it."

"Goodbye, you addict!" And then he left.

That was the end. And it happened very easy. The only thing I told him was that I visited a therapist and I am starting my therapy that includes antidepressants, anxiolytics, and regular sessions. That scared him to death. So apparently, I was a drug addict. A slut. A police whore. I became someone whom he couldn't control anymore. Someone who wants to think, heal, grow, talk to therapists, read self-help books, take medications; that was not going in his favour. That was it.

I slept well that night, alone and strangely at peace. When I woke up, I was missing him like crazy, but continued my day. I did my make-up and hair, put some pearls and sunglasses on. It was a nice summer day. And when I stepped outside my building, I looked around. Everything had a bit brighter color than yesterday. And I could take a deep breath. Next, it was time to breathe out.

That Day When
I Met Francesco

"And I love you like a song

Yes, I love you

And without you, I wander."

Everywhere by Paolo Nutini

I was not really on the 'Eat, pray, love' path, but I had chosen Rome for my Postdoctoral studies. Using my inheritance, I could afford to live a decent life in the Italian capital. I didn't have a specific limit on the credit card, but I gave my best to be smart with it. I would sometimes make a withdrawal and just keep it in one of my books. My "back-up" that nobody knew about.

It was a very cold day in November, cold for Rome anyway, and the forecast was saying that some snow might fall. I was leaving my flat that was close to the Institute building. I was enjoying the fresh air, my boots on the pavement and the favorite part–picking up coffee to-go. I was listening to Marvin Gaye on my phone and drinking my first coffee, while walking to the rhythm of the song; that was the best part of my day. And a cigarette. Yep, back then I was smoking. And that morning one was so good, it was so enjoyable, so calming. There was nothing better than having a coffee with a cigarette.

I entered the office at the Institute, turned on my computer, and there it was, an email from my supervisor. I do not know why, but she just loved to write emails with red letters; at least to me. I have never asked her why; and I will never know why. Some people are just in your life for a season, and you do not need to know everything about their behaviour. Even if your job is to observe human behaviour. Some members of the species are just not interesting enough to be observed.

That red email was informing me that we have a new subject in our case. A volunteer, who always wanted to know more about Neuroscience but never found an opportunity, and now wants to be a part of a study that interests him. My team was collecting fMRIs of the subject's brains, before and after they had a meditation about a specific person. If telepathy really exists, and I strongly believed that it does, I wanted to know which parts of the brain and which hormones are involved in it. Subjects would think about the specific person with and without meeting with him or her, and we also took fMRIs from the specific persons that were in the thoughts of the subject. Blood was taken from both types of experimental groups, the ones that were thinking about their subject and the subject itself, so that we can monitor the hormone levels.

I loved the kind of people who wanted to participate. My research heavily depended on the people volunteering and giving their precious time to us, to contribute to science. I had to meet the new subject at 11 am, in the office of my supervisor and then do an interview and run some initial tests. *This will be a long day,* I thought. But more subjects, more data, and hopefully that paper which will bring me to the end of my stay in Rome. And then back to the US. I did not plan to go back to LA, but I did want to go back to Cali.

My closest colleague and flatmate, Steffi, and me were so tired from our shifts at the Institute. It felt like we were there for 48 hours. Oh, wait, we were! I went to my apartment, just to change my clothes. For too long I had been focused on the work phone, waiting for supervisor calls, emails, texts; so I needed a break from it, if only for an hour. I am far away from being able to sleep. That's why that coffee with cigarette felt so damn good!

I met with our new case study in the office of my supervisor since she was at the conference that week. Everyone tries to use the generous space and comfort of her corner office overlooking the Castel Sant'Angelo and Vatican. She might be an evil woman, but she for sure fought for what she wanted. She fought for her passion towards the research in her lab and being co-founder of this Institute.

When I was searching for a place where I would do my Postdoctoral time, she was my top choice. She was still in prime-time energy-wise, she was good looking and successful. She was the example. I wanted to be her when I grew up. Her research on sleeping and how different factors influence our REM and NREM phases, was so interesting. Currently, her lab, including me, wants to learn more about narcolepsy. She was also very much interested in my proposal that we should know more about telepathy. Luckily, I did connect the science with the belief, and with that she didn't look at me as a completely strange individual, besides the fact that I *was* one.

The current volunteer wanted to be in this study, but during the interview with me, he stated that he has a family history of dementia and Alzheimer's disease. He wanted to know what his cognitive results were. Since there were some indications of the connection between dementia and narcolepsy, I decided to do blood tests, MRI, EEG, genome sequencing and see what is happening with him. Of course, before I handed him over to the nurses, I informed my boss; nothing without her consent! I proposed to include the volunteer in both the narcolepsy and telepathy study. And I was dreading to get the reply about my proposition. Even though she was my idol and an example, which is what I thought while observing her from US, now that I am in her lab, I am starting to get a picture of the real her.

After getting green light from my boss, the subject was admitted to the Institute's clinic. Afterwards, both Steffi and I decided to go to the bar across the street and have a night cap. Our research was failing us so much in our private life. Meaning we didn't have one, our life was our work. We did everything that we told our test subjects and patients not to do, because work/life balance is important. Truthfully, I did not want that kind of life. I was starting to get miserable, with an idol that turned into a horrible nightmare. Let's be honest, she was using every chance to put me down and show me how much I didn't know and will never know. I was lonely. Truly lonely. I missed my family; I missed my friends. Yes, I had Steffi, but she was crazy enough to try a different Italian guy almost every night. Not my rhythm.

The bar was full, and we just asked the waiter for two shots of tequila and two beers. We will stand and drink. No problem. That is what young people on Friday night should do: dance and have an awesome time. We got our shots and beers, then there was one free spot at the bar, so we settled there and continued with more shots. That worked towards the goal of having some fun, since I started to dance and laugh and enjoy my time with Steffi. Until one Italian, as charming as he was, stumbled over to that gorgeous flatmate of mine and asked her for a dance. I found myself immediately feeling as lonely as before the alcohol numbed my brain and heart, and asked for a glass of water to dilute all the drinks.

Bonnie Tyler and 'Total Eclipse of the Heart' started and all in the bar began slow dancing and singing. That's a song that still makes me shiver. I have listened to it a lot, post-Mauricio, and it symbolizes the ending of a very important part of my life.

Then I saw him. White shirt, big smile, hazelnut eyes with a blue sparkle (God knows how I saw that), coming towards me. I turned to see if there was some gorgeous blonde behind me and he is headed towards her. But he stopped in front of me and asked, "Why is this beautiful lady alone and not dancing?" He offered his hand, inviting me to join him to the dance floor.

"Well, I guess now I am not alone, and I am about to dance." I had to say something quickly, not to look like as paralyzed by his smile as I was. His eyes locked me.

I had no confidence what-so-ever in dancing at that moment, but with my hand in his, there was an electrical shock that made me surrender to his moves and let him lead me. We were moving slowly. I could smell plums on his neck and see part of his aura that was shining bright, sky blue. I was mesmerized by his embrace. I guess those two minutes of dancing made me less alone than the whole year in Rome. By the end of the song, he looked in my eyes and smiled. *Oh, no! The smile!*

"What is your name?" He asked.

Usually I would lie, to be careful with strangers. I would say Britney, or Jessica, or something like that, but I just said, "Masha." *Damn!*

"Nice to meet you, Masha. My name is…"

"…Francesco." I have no idea how I knew that name, but I must admit that I had it in my head from the moment I saw him.

"Wow, it's amazing! You guessed my name! I like that." Again, that smile.

I looked down and begged for Steffi to appear. I just wanted to go home now. I was scared, not of him, but of myself. I was standing in front of probably the actual manifestation of my ideal man, drunk after a 48 hour-long shift, and I could not think straight. Going home was the best decision. I was not sure what I would do. Go with him? Out of Rome? Never to be seen again?

"I am so sorry, but I need to go home. I need to sleep. It has been a long week for me."

"I understand, and I can sense that you are tired." He can *sense* that I am tired? I must look horrible.

"Thank you for understanding. It was nice to meet you, Francesco."

"No, let me escort you home. You are not in a condition to go alone."

"I will go with a taxi, don't worry."

"No, no, I insist."

And it was good that he came with me, since I fell asleep in the car and could barely exit. Francesco managed to make me tell him the code for the building entrance, and the floor, and the number of the apartment. He unlocked it and carried me inside. He placed me in the bed, without touching any of my clothes, he covered me and left a bucked beside my bed. All I could say was thank you. And then I blacked out. I didn't feel when he kissed my forehead.

∗ ∗ ∗

In the morning, I saw the blanket on the couch; so, he slept here to make sure I was okay. He left me two tablets of ibuprofen and water on my nightstand. He wrote on a post-it.

Hi, Masha. I am happy that we met. I could tell that you are a soul that I want to know more. Please rest and feel better. This is my number, 06-2468880. Please call me, Francesco.

I knew that Italians were flirty and can overwhelm you with compliments. Believe me, I have seen that through Steffi. But this felt different, it felt sincere, even though there was no logic behind it. This did not make any sense. I could end up with a very bad heartbreak. Another one. After Mauricio, I was mainly having one-night stands. Which was okay, since my career was unpredictable and could require moving a lot, changing cities, countries, continents.

In my 20s, I decided that career was the most important thing, and that no man should be an obstacle to it. My mother brainwashed me with the concept too. She herself never worked and because of that, she insisted that I never forget that men are not there to be financially more dominant over me. Men are fun, replaceable, and useful. I am the one who makes *myself* happy, with my success, my friends, and my travels. Could I blame my mother for all those teachings? *Absolutely.* But the truth is, I made all my decisions, and I liked being successful and independent. Meeting Mauricio brought a perfect lesson that I had to learn. Men are distractions. Men were not for me at this moment in my life. And if anyone asks, Francesco could be just the product of my long hours and lots of drinks. It's possible that I have never met him. He was just my imagination.

Minus the post-it. Which I took, opened the drawer, not the first, but the second one of my nightstand. The one that I don't open frequently, and there you go. *Gone.* I took the pills. No evidence of anyone trespassing here. Next stop, shower. Science cannot wait.

* * *

Everybody deserves someone who goes out of their way to make it obvious that they would do anything and go to the Moon and back to show them how much they want them in their life. I started to believe that I am not among those lucky women who meet a guy who gives everything for them.

I had a friend back in LA, who was among the lucky ladies to meet a guy who would do anything for her. She would do whatever she wanted; he was okay with it. I'm not joking. They got married, they have kids, he's still as in love with her as the first day they met. And often, I'm left wondering, *what does she have, that I do not?* Am I ever going to meet a guy who would care for me like that?

After finishing the shift at the Institute, I was exhausted, from the night before, and from all the bad Western blots. I just wanted to go home and shower, eat a soup and sleep. Steffi and I were thinking about which movie to watch when we both saw Francesco leaning on a motorcycle in front of the Institute building, in a black leather jacket. Waiting for me.

Who knows how long he was waiting, since there isn't a specific time when I leave from work. Especially if I sleep on the office couch. I didn't use his number; I *did not* open the second drawer. I had not made any contact with him. But there he was. Dressed in black, all devil-like, and all God damn beautiful.

"Well Steffi, there will be no movie with you tonight…" I said, my stomach felt warm and filled with butterflies.

"I thought you would say that." Steffi managed to respond, not moving her eyes from the picture of Francesco waving at us.

* * *

All I remember about the following days is blue. And his eyes had a blue sparkle and changed color from hazelnut to gray, whenever the sky changed its color. I remember his dark hair and big smile. I remember his blue shirt and strong handshake. I remember hearing the echo of his name in my head, *Francesco*. And the way he pronounced my name. Sharp and soft at the same time.

Blue, a lot of blue. I hadn't noticed snow falling outside, a phenomenon that made some people happy. I didn't notice the slippery streets on the way back home. And I did not notice that I have smoked the whole package of cigarettes throughout the night.

I haven't slept, I wasn't tired. I was just thinking, *what the hell just happened to me?* What have I become in the last hours? I am someone who now cannot imagine a day without those eyes looking at me. I've become a person that I have told myself I would never become. *Again.* I never ever wanted to fall in love. *Again.* I did not want to be a prisoner of those feelings. *Again.* But with his smile and my hand in his… All my plans were falling apart.

We spent several nights together in a row. And I had to wait 15 days until I could see Francesco again. He told me he needed to travel to Napoli to sell some of his paintings. I had to occupy my mind for two weeks, I made myself available for any tasks that my supervisor had. She wanted to perform an experiment where the subject would not be allowed to sleep for 48 hours, without any coffee or other stimulants. Then they would give blood to test their hormones. Food and water were available. I had to follow the subjects and their tests, and the experiments were going with several subjects at the same time. *A perfect distraction!* Except, it was not. I was thinking about his plum-like smell, every second of every minute.

* * *

(Three months later)

"I love you, M. Ti amo! Really, with all my being. Don't ever doubt it! I would give everything for you! You are the one."

I was crashing into his arms, melting my soul into his chest. He knew exactly which words to say, which buttons to push to make me surrender completely. His dark brown hair felt so good in my hand while he was kissing me. That night I allowed him to paint my body. He placed me naked on the canvas and started to make a border around me. I quickly became a fire that couldn't be extinguished. When the white canvas with my body shape in blue was done, we made love. That piece of art was sold for half a million euros. Francesco was planning that money to go towards a house for us. I could not stop smiling, imagining our future together.

* * *

He was kissing my back.

"Please, let me kiss you." I begged.

He refused; he did not want me to see his face. My dress was halfway unzipped and with one move he removed it completely off my body. His hand was playing with the band of my panties, while his other hand was grabbing my hair and pulling it, giving him space to suck on my neck.

I was moaning to the rhythm of his bites. I wanted him so badly. His fingers slipped inside of me, and I was his.

"How much do you want to see my face?" He asked while playing with me, his fingers pushing so deep and hard.

I could not say anything but, a desperate, "Please." With his last, most intense thrust, he made me scream. Then he pulled my hair so hard that he turned my head towards my right shoulder, so I could look at him.

I scream again. But this time, it was not a scream of pleasure. His face was fire, disformed lava. His eyes dark, like tourmaline. He made a sound that was like a laughter.

"Now, you know. You are mine, Masha. You gave yourself to me. And I will always be with you. "

My body felt stiff, there was no more movement or sound left in it. Tears were falling down my cheeks. When he got closer again to kiss me, I felt like I become fire too. And now, my fire is mixing with his.

Then I woke up, completely covered in sweat. The window was open, and the curtain was moving with the light breeze of the summer night. I looked to my left; Francesco was sleeping calmly. I went to the kitchen to take a glass of water. And then I prayed.

I never knew the exact words of the main prayers from the Bible, even though my parents were somewhat religious. I tried to resist it, especially going down the scientific path. But tonight, I was searching for the words and I started with, "Our Father, who art in Heaven…" Then I just cried. I did not know why I felt like I did. Why my dream was so real and terrifying. Was it a warning? A premonition? If God was listening to me, if he was sensing my soul, I did not have to say anything anymore, or know anything, he would understand how much I needed him.

Mysterious Ways
Of Our Lives

"You are imperfect, you are wired for struggle, but you are worthy of love and belonging."

Brené Brown

We had days where we both would be in Francesco's studio. While he was painting, I was reading my scientific papers. But most of the time, my eyes would be on him. I would be observing his strong arms, lean body, abs, lips…. Ah, those lips would say the most beautiful words, when they wanted to. And a sharp, concentrated look on the canvas. *Eyes of God*, I thought. Then I remembered my dream. And how, for a few weeks now, I was attending liturgies in the church close by. I couldn't explain why, but I felt completely secure and safe when I was there. My dream was telling me that something bad would happen. That was my definite conclusion, and I could not shake it off.

But being with Francesco left me feeling safe, too. I hated when he would go on his trips, to search for clientele. I would tell him that there is no need for that, we were in Rome, the art is here! He did not need to travel anywhere. But his trips were more and more frequent, and somehow all of them were to Napoli. I asked to come once, but he found some excuse. Like he would be sleeping in a very cheap hotel and he does not want me to feel uncomfortable. But, as soon he sells something again, we could afford to stay somewhere nice and I would join him.

It made me wonder, where is the money from that one painting that he did sell? The one that was worth half a million dollars and was created with passion that was invested into it by both of us. My brain went into so many different directions, so many different scenarios. We said that money goes towards building our dream home, but I didn't know where that money was. I felt uncomfortable asking about it. It was his first sale, and I am just his girlfriend, so I retracted myself from further investigation. However, at that very moment, while watching him work, my thoughts that something weird was happening would not leave me alone. So, I stretched my body on the bed, a 'change the position and the thoughts will change' kind of moto. Francesco's attention went towards me immediately.

"What is happening? Are you tired?" He had a smirk on his face.

"A little bit. I am bored with these papers; I've read them like 100 times. I don't know why I try to memorise them when the committee for the grant will be focused on my non-existing results, anyways."

"You did such an amazing job with all your work so far. I am not an expert, but I saw how you talked about it, how people listened and were interested to ask questions, every time when you gave a talk. You did that, Masha! Current results or not, the point is that you have a goal, you have an idea. And if you get that grant, great. If not, there will be another opportunity where your vision will be recognized."

I was not into pep talks, but I needed this one. He came to the bed and hugged me, which melted all my insecurities. I don't know how he did that. He was able to look me in the eyes, and just with that, elevate my vibration. Sometimes, I wanted to perform experiments on him and myself. I felt that he could read my mind, and that our thoughts had a distinct path between us; we would be a perfect case study. And even though, I never said anything about that out loud, it was on my to-do-list. As soon as I had my own money and have more freedom in my project. My supervisor would need to accept some of my suggestions then.

Francesco didn't talk much about his family, or for that matter, his feelings in depth. He would say he loves me, or that he cares for me. However, his thinking process about many things continued being mystery to me. I could only guess his mood by the way he was approaching his canvas that day. If he was waking up, and love would be on his mind, the canvas would become brighter, lighter colors would appear on it. You could feel the love coming from it. Once, he wrote me a poem and he read it to me. It was sunset, we were sitting on the balcony with a glass of wine, and the words were kissing my body; that's how it felt. I honestly thought I could survive from that evening for at least a month! I had a smile on my face the next day. Work was easy, I was flying across the rooms, and my flatmate was really annoyed, especially when I would play "Moon River" five thousand times on repeat. I said I could live a month because I had to. Franco left Rome for some painter's retreat. He said he paid a lot of money for it, and he needed to go. I assumed that money must have been from his first sale.

A month later, I got his letter.

"Amore mio,

I hope you are doing well. I had really nice progress with my technique this month and had a very nice time. The mountain air is magical. I went climbing with my colleagues. Me! Can you imagine? But I survived, and it felt like an achievement. I also met lots of my companions, painters, and I think I will stay for a bit longer. They plan to continue the work, even after the retreat is over.

Don't worry, I won't forget about you. Ever!

Every time I am on the top of the mountain, I look at the sky and I think I see you, smiling at me from above. Watching over me. I do not want to lose you. It took so much time to find you! Where have you been all my life? Hiding away.

I will see you soon.

Take care.

Con amore, Il tuo, Franco."

I wished that I would hear more from him during that first month. But the following period was even worse. For the next few months, my phone did not show calls or messages from him, no emails, nothing… Of course, I was worried. Thousands of thoughts went through my head. *Is he okay? Are we okay? Maybe he did forget about me. Maybe he doesn't want to be with me.* Some mornings, I thought that it may be better to continue my life without him. I still loved him. With all my heart. And it was painful to wake up knowing that I would not see him that day. Some mornings I called in sick. Some days I was angry and bitter. But most of the time, I was numb and empty. *How could he? Why?*

I was going to bed thinking of him, waking up thinking of him. When I prayed, I prayed for him. Sometimes I felt like not going to the lab, just because I wanted to daydream about him, to imagine him being beside me, loving me, touching me, kissing me. My inner world felt so much better than my reality. With all that was happening, I also got a letter saying that I did not get the grant for my research. I felt trapped. Stuck. Cornered. And dark thoughts started creeping in.

* * *

One weekend I decided to let Steffi take charge of me and she organized a weekend out of the city, on the seaside. It felt nice to change the environment and at the same time to be away from everything that reminded me of him. Even though he was everywhere I looked. The way the wind touched me, the sand on my feet, the smell of the sea. The heart has a mind of its own and I really tried to heal it. But I could not fight it, not at that moment. While sitting at the beach, with gloomy clouds over me, looking at the waves. I was thinking, *did he really abandon me? Just like that? Is this it?*

Francesco was unique and with all his misty and gloomy moods, I wanted him. So badly. I really hoped that he would come back. Maybe I did not give him enough before? Maybe I need to be more involved? Does love really have to hurt that much?

In the evening, after a good portion of time trying to feel good with my friend and some random guys that Steffi had fun with, I would return to my part of the villa, and I cried. I cried until I was completely dry. And then some more.

Was this really the end with Francesco?

In a castle

There is not even a shadow of you besides me...

You are not even a ghost...

And I long for your embrace...

For your kiss...

Such a pain without you,

Such a sorrow.

It hurts to be apart,

Two halves separated.

Was it your wish or mine?

I cannot remember the fact,

Reality is not my thing, you know.

I live in a castle,

I live in a dream,

Wish no hard words, no problems.

I want you back,

Now.

I want your soul attached to mine,

Again.

Is it a sin, to want that?

You promised me, a long time ago,

That we will live our dream together.

And then you left.

Was it because of me or you?

I cannot remember the fact,

Reality is not my thing, you know.

I live in the Source,

I live in the Optimism.

And this, this empty bed confuses me.

Because I live in a dream,

Because I live in a dream.

(Masha's diary entry)

* * *

Everyone who has ever loved would tell you that there is no greater feeling than love. They would tell you that love is the only law in the Universe. Everyone who ever loved would say that surrendering to it is life's purpose.

These people would say that there is no greater pain than that of losing the person you love. Or losing love itself. Love that was so deeply engraved into the soul and then suddenly disappeared.

How love turned into some other emotion. How, when you look in the mirror, you see a person who you were not yesterday. Yesterday, when love was the only thing on your mind. You do not have one bad day. Every day is a bad day.

* * *

(Two months later)

I woke up with a huge hangover and a massive headache. Apparently, sometime during the night, in all that fun that I had with my tears, sleeping pills and wine, I managed to trip over my vanity chair. I fell backwards and hit my head so hard that at first I thought I broke my skull. After the initial shock, I got up and I was fine. I had two ibuprofens and a shower. Every drop of water that dripped on my head was like a knife. So, I cried some more.

When I looked at myself in the mirror afterwards, it was a scary picture. I must have lost 15 pounds, I had bags under my eyes, dark ones, and my hair was lifeless, and its color looked like a washed-out brown dress.

"What are you doing to yourself?" I yelled at my image in the mirror.

My whole life was doing a downward spiral since my father died. My family fell apart, Mauricio, heart attack, moving to Europe, escaping the old. I didn't like what I do, I stopped liking the way I was living altogether. I wanted to leave my own *skin*. Maybe it was time to move again. That was what I did. If life felt unbearable, I was leaving. Moving to a new location so I could refresh my emotions. If Francesco does not come back, if he is not the love of my life as I felt that he was, I need to leave this country. I need to move. *Again*.

I did not want to wait for Steffi. I got dressed and went out to have coffee alone in some coffee shop. To journal, to think. I was going down the street and one shop particularly was fitting my mood, and they were playing Debussy. *Perfection*! I ordered a cappuccino and closed my eyes to soak in the melody, matching the beating of my heart with the song, Suite Bergamasque, L. 75: III. Clair de Lune - Giovanni Umberto Battel.

How can somebody be so right for you and at the same time run from you as fast and as far away as they can?

* * *

A week after, he appeared in front of my building. Rome was wet from the rain, and so were my eyes.

"Franco!" I ran into his embrace. I stayed there for a long time. Until he pulled me away from him. His eyes were red and swollen. I pulled him again into a hug, but again, he shifted away. The only thought in my head was, *he's here.*

"How are you?" I finally asked.

"Good, I guess. I shouldn't be here really. I'm all sweaty from the travel and wet from the rain…"

"Come on, Franco! It wouldn't be the first time you showered at my place." I smiled, but my soul was burning. Something was wrong.

"No. I just wanted to say hi. See you tomorrow, mi amore." After that, he left. My soul was on fire, my instincts were overworking. *Something is wrong. He is not my Franco anymore.*

Roman Love Story

"He's more myself than I am. Whatever our souls are made of, his and mine are the same."

Wuthering Heights by Emily Brontë

One cold winter day, approximately the year after I met Francesco, he called me in the middle of the day. He sounded like something urgent was happening. I was in the middle of my experiment, the subject was monitored with EEG, and it needed at least 6 more hours until the end.

Francesco was yelling on the phone. "I need you now! I need your support! If you do not come now, I will never speak to you again!"

I really thought it was one of his usual panic modes, when he was in his creative phase. And it would pass after we talk briefly on the phone, but he did not let me talk. He continued yelling, he started to cry hysterically. And then hung up. Cold air passed through me. I felt like I was talking with Mauricio again. It was the same type of threats, and yelling. I shook my head and told myself that this is not Mauricio, this is a man who loves me and who just had a problem. *I can help him.*

I asked my technician to do me a favour and stay until the end of the experiment, with the promise that I would do whatever she needed for the whole next week, and then I went to Franco's studio.

As a scientist, I was devastated. Maybe that data would prove my theory about the connection of two human beings. I needed as many recordings of brain activity as possible, but the woman inside of me was worried and couldn't wait to be close to Franco. I must admit that lately these episodes started to get more frequent, so maybe that is why I had the Mauricio vibes. But I loved Franco, and when he was away it showed me that I really am in love with him.

On the other hand, after his return, Francesco was not as he was before, deeply loving, and crazy just to be with me. He was nervous, often lost in his thoughts, or literally gone who knows where. We were basically living together in his studio, so I was feeling his absence much more intensely than if I would retreat to my apartment. When we found out that I was expecting, the decision was made that I leave my place and move in with him. My hormones were so high, and they influenced my thinking. I was dedicated to fix any problem that Francesco had before the baby comes. Steffi was trying to bring some sense into me, telling me that I have to take care of myself first, but I was in love and I was expecting a kid with the man I love. Everything else did not matter.

The taxi left me in front of his building, and I felt cold air pushing me away again. Chills creeped all over my body. I didn't want to go in. But here I was. The main door of the building was unlocked. Romans just took forever to repair things. Reaching the fourth floor, Franco's door was unlocked, too. As I opened the door the smell of marijuana and stale air overwhelmed me. I was trying to find my way through the smoke.

"Franco, it's me. Where are you?" I was yelling and coughing at the same time. "Franco, please tell me where you are."

The living room was a mess, beer bottles everywhere. Finished joints lying all over. I was spending a few days at the Institute, monitoring my experiment's subjects. Plus, Steffi wanted me to spend some time with her, some girlfriend time that we did not do for quite a while. This mess had time to accumulate. But it also looked like he had some company. There were some open books on the floor. His paintings had cuts through the middle. I was shaking.

Maybe someone else is here and Franco is hurt? Should I call the police? The bedroom was empty. The bed was not made and everything smelled like vomit. The bathroom was shocking! The tub was filled with dirty dishes, and they were swimming in water and some bubbles of detergent. It smelled like fungi growth and desperation. Finally, I reached the kitchen, and there he was. In front of the canvas, painting it all black with a joint in his mouth. He looked fine, he *seemed* fine. When he saw me, he put a big smile on his face.

"All my work up until now is crap. I want to make a better statement. And I think I can do it. I don't want to depend on those idiots from the gallery. I will sell on my own. Look, this will be a black hole. The ultimate goal! The divine! What do you think, baby?"

All the fear that I have felt, all the worry, turned to anger. I wanted to scream, I wanted to hit him, to smash his canvas against the wall. He scared me, and for what? Another one of his crazy artistic panic attacks.

"What do you want from me?" I tried to ask it calmly.

"Oh, yes! I was panicking, because my mother comes to visit me tomorrow, and I have all those dishes that I haven't done, because of all the inspiration that I have! So, I need your help with that. Can you please, baby? I am scared to see how my mother will react if she would see the place in this mess!"

He came to me and took my head, pulled it up towards his face and kissed me. I did not say a word. But I did not kiss back. I was so angry that I started to cry.

"Oh, no! Per favore, non piangere! Why are you so sad?"

Even if I wanted to tell him how I felt, he was too stoned to understand. I didn't comprehend how he can think this is normal behaviour. Who is this man? What happened to Francesco? The pieces of his personality do not fit anymore into, well, anything. There was damage done while he was gone, but he never wanted to talk about it or to admit to anything. I was surrendering to the situation and hurting. I knew that I was hurting. And I did not want to admit this to anyone. Even admitting it to myself was a half-way thing.

"I go to start the dishes."

"Thank you, amore mio!" He smiled at me like everything was okay and entirely normal.

"Yeah." I turned away. I closed myself in the guest toilet, the only untouched place, and I cried for at least half an hour. Then I wiped my tears and went to the bathroom to start the dishes.

* * *

I remembered the song 'Coming home to you' by Luca Stavos and that beautiful evening at Piazza Navona. Franco and I were going to a dinner and we were walking by a musician on the street. We stopped to hear his beautiful playing, so many people had paused to listen to him. Franco asked me for a dance, and we were laughing and kissing and applauding at the end. Seeing Franco that evening in a grey suit, in any suit for that matter, made me see another side of him. He was beautiful, but there was an additional confidence, his step was mature, he looked like he could achieve anything in his cape. That was the true color of him that I was waiting to see for a long time! I missed strong, loving, joyful Franco. And he was back!

I was completely sure that I fell even more in love that evening, seeing him dressed like that. Happy like that. I was dressed in a black summer dress, perfect for a hot summer evening. Perfect for a romantic Roman summer night.

"Where do we go?" I asked.

"To my cousin's restaurant, but I want to make a stop before that, to check something."

"Okay." I could not connect the suit with his cousin's restaurant but why not? We are fancy tonight, just because the night is beautiful.

He looked a bit nervous, like he had to sell some of his important pieces. I turned to see if there was something in the car that I haven't noticed, but the car was empty. From time to time, he would look at me and smile, but beads of sweat were accumulating on his forehead.

"Are you alright?" I asked as gentle as possible.

"Absolutely!" He smiled and took my hand to kiss it. The sky was clear, the Moon was full. Full and loving. *It really is a beautiful night,* I thought.

Francesco stopped the car close to St. Angelo Bridge, then we walked towards it. A couple was on the bridge taking selfies. Some young people where drinking and smoking and listening to music, having a good time.

"Masha, since you came into my life, nothing else is as important anymore." Franco looked deep into my eyes. "Except seeing *you* happy and making *you* happy. I don't know what I did to deserve this. To deserve you, for you to love me. If anything, I consider myself unworthy of the love of a woman like you. Gorgeous, pretty, smart, good, calm… the best. You take the heaviness from my shoulders, and you must have been sent by angels. I do not have much to give you, but I will try to make a better life for both of us. I will work hard. I will love hard. I want to be worthy of you. Because when I look into your eyes, it is the only place I can see the future. Masha Boki," then he went down on one knee, "will you please make me forever your knight, that will fight for you and us, the three of us, every day for the rest of our lives?"

My eyes were wet already when he started to talk. I knew where everything leads. And I wanted to be his with my whole body and soul. I could not imagine any other life but a life with Francesco. No matter what. For better and for worse.

"Yes, yes, of course I will marry you! I love you!"

He got up and kissed me. I felt like I was being transported to another Universe. His kisses could do that. Then he took out his phone from his pocket and played "Moon River", the only instrumental from Rieu that I loved, and then took the ring out. It was round, a ruby in yellow gold.

"It belonged to my grandmother; we will fix the size." But it fit perfectly. I was speechless. Is that why his mother was coming to his studio? After placing the ring on my finger, he said, *I love you.*

Until this day, that was my most beautiful night. Francesco knew me. He knew where and how to touch me. How to put my hair behind my ear and then whisper gentle words until I started to sigh. He showed me what it means to make love. To kiss my upper lip like it was the biggest treasure in the world. To pass his hand from my neck to my hip line to make my body tremble. It was magnificent to be loved by him.

The week after, I finally met the whole family. His mother organized a big celebration for the engagement of her son. We ended up telling everyone that we are expecting, and the engagement celebration turned into the celebration of the future baby. He did not leave my side the whole time.

I was never happier than that week. I took time off from the Institute and I was supported by my supervisor, believe it or not. She was happy for me. Franco took her breath away for sure when he was visiting, so with his influence she gave me a generous two weeks off. *To have my well-deserved rest,* she said those words herself. Steffi was happy for me too, even though there was always a carefully hidden suspicious look; taking care that Francesco does not hurt me in any way. I loved her for loving me and being my friend. But I told her that there was no need to worry. Everything will be amazing!

* * *

For the next few weeks, I was in Franco's, *our,* apartment and while he was producing brilliance and his art was progressing every day, I was reading and learning Italian with the occasional look-up of some new scientific paper. In the evening, we would usually cook and eat dinner on the small balcony. After doing the dishes, Franco would poor some red wine for himself and tea for me, and we would chat about the future.

He had plans, lots of them. He wanted to buy and renovate the entire building where he lived, so that we could get more space. A separate studio for him, and a study room for me.

"And an additional room for a baby." He would add, so relaxed like he was always waiting for this moment.

"I want to have kids with you, I want to be father of your kids."

His voice made me feel safe, I could feel when he was telling the truth, and he *was* telling the truth at that moment.

After finishing his wine, Franco stood up and asked for my hand. He pulled me into a hug so strong that I could barely breathe.

"Hey, are you okay?" I asked.

"I love you, Masha. *So* much!" He looked into my eyes and smiled. "God was good when he gave me your love."

I felt so much in love with him myself. Francesco was my soulmate in the whole meaning of that word. We grew so much together in just a few months. We pushed each other's buttons, witnessed each other's meltdowns, had a period of horrible insecurity, strange disconnect and distance, just to make our relationship stronger. I felt blessed that I could feel the love I have felt those months.

He gave me a long and passionate kiss. When I gathered my breath, I told him that I love him too. I felt his soul entering my body, and my soul entering his. It was one moment in time with Francesco, my fiancée, that felt like a creation of a completely new Universe. Our Universe.

* * *

It was a sunny, blue-sky day in Rome. Getting ready for work felt easier than most days, since the morning sickness did not kick in quite yet. And most days I was waking up already feeling like I was ready to vomit. I managed to put the whole piece of toast in my stomach and some fruits and a bit of orange juice. Francesco was still in bed, trying to wake up and start his work a bit earlier, so that we can have a nice picnic in the evening. I was craving to spend more time outside. I kissed Franco, we wished each other a great day, and I was already at the door when he called me back. I turned. His face was bright, his eyes were smiling.

"I love you." He said.

"I love you too." I smiled.

His eyes were a deep, blue, grey; suddenly all the colors were mixed in there. And all those colors were flowing towards me. Hugging me. Kissing me. Telling me that they would stay with me to protect me.

"Bye, Franco."

"Bye, Masha."

On the way back from the Institute, I bought a few oranges, and some flowers. I was looking forward to spending an evening outside with Francesco. So, when the apartment door was open, and when the first picture that I saw was a body surrounded by blood, all the oranges and daisies dropped towards the floor. There was a scream. And then another one when I picked up cold, bloody knife from the floor.

There was nothing that I could do. Except kiss his lifeless body and pray that this is just one of my dreams, one of the nightmares, and soon I will wake up and find Francesco sleeping beside me in the bed. I was still praying while I was sitting in the cold, police cell, waiting for the lawyer, my mother and the family psychiatrist, Luca. Even when they arrived, taking care of my release, transporting me to the hotel room, and while my mother and Steffi washed off the blood of my body, I was still praying. *Please God, give him back to me.*

Not Happily
Ever After

"Though lovers be lost, love shall not."

Dylan Thomas

Researching was going badly. I literally did not see the point in doing what I was doing. The most frustrating part was that my supervisor did not want to allow me to perform my own experiments anymore. I tried to argue that I felt much better, and I was ready to work again, but she was ruthless. It was her way and no others. She did not see that I was better. And even if I hated her for that, she was right.

When I was released from prison, my mother was persistent on bringing me back to LA. I was just not ready to go back. To leave all the memories with Francesco behind, his family that I just started to know. My mother didn't know that I was pregnant. All my sickness, she concluded, was because I was grieving. And I *was* grieving. My soul was crying when I could not. After a few days, I convinced my mother that I need more time, before I returned to the US. So, I spent a month trying to exit the bed, crying, crying some more, getting on antidepressants, which Luca has chosen carefully since he knew my situation and we wanted to be sure that there was no danger to the baby. But the medications didn't work, I was in a really dark place. One evening all I did was lay on the floor of my bathroom, smelly, not showered, vomiting up the whole cake that I had eaten. This was my rock bottom.

Yes, I reached the low that I thought I would never allow to happen. Tears were coming down my chocolate-vomit-smeared face. I was ready to die. And the bottle of pills was just right there. I was done vomiting, there is no way that I could do it anymore. So, if I took all of them and fell asleep, maybe I would never wake up. No one would find me for days. Everyone left me alone now. That would be it.

I turned my head towards the pills, and tears started to fall more and more. I thought of Francesco's soft hair, of his touches on my body. And then I thought about the life that was growing inside of me.

I would not be able to be a single mother, trying to navigate between LA and Rome. At least I would have a reason to leave this stupid Postdoctoral program.

As the thoughts were coming and going, so incoherent and most of them just out of rage, I managed to wash my face and change my shirt. I decided to try to sleep. I took one sleeping pill. *Good girl.*

* * *

His red eyes were looking at me. He chained my arms and legs onto the wheel of fortune. "La vie en Rose" was playing in the background by a midget with clown shoes.

"Tell me that you love me." The red-eyed creature ordered me.

"Who are you?" I was crying and begging to be released.

"How dare you?" He asked while fire was coming out of his mouth. "I gave you everything! I made this world for you! I made you my queen! And you dare ask me who I am?"

There were creatures flying around, some bowing to me, another painting the moment. I realized that I am in a grotesque dream of mine, where my husband is the Devil himself.

"Please don't hurt me, the baby…"

"That baby is also mine; I decide what happens to it."

"And what will happen to me?"

He approached me. Coming so close that I could feel the fire in his eyes. "That is up to the underworld rules…" And he spun the wheel. I was spinning, and spinning and feeling sick, until I woke up from the nightmare…

I was vomiting in my bed, and the pain in my lower abdomen was harsh. When I looked, the bed was soaked not only in my vomit but also in my blood… My baby did not survive.

* * *

I didn't know how to cope with the situation, it was bad from every angle. The pills were not working, I even stopped taking them, since I would just feel nothing and sleep all day. Maybe that was for the best, maybe not, but at that moment I was just able to cry, scream and cry some more.

The police came one day to inform that they connected Francesco's murder with a local drug circle, apparently Francesco owed them a lot of money. My question was, *for what*, he was not using drugs, except the occasional joint. I did not get many answers. The story goes much deeper, and was connected with Franco's family. He wanted to save his cousin from the mafia, and he needed to pay the dept. *Oh, my good Francesco, why did you not tell me? Why did you not try to involve the police?* If his cousin really wanted out, there had to be another way. Who knows what he witnessed all these months. Especially when he said that he was on the retreat, that was probably when he was negotiating. Now, his behaviour makes sense.

I decided to write a letter to Francesco, that I would never be able to send.

My dearest Francesco,

I miss you. I miss when I do not get a message from you. I miss you when you do not call me. I miss your tender words. I miss your smile. Your beautiful hair. I miss your touch. And all those moments when you made me laugh. Simply, I miss you.

It has been two months since I have seen you. I am desperate. I cannot stand another day without you. All the effort to live and exist without you here, just doesn't work. I still miss you. I miss your face, your hug, the touch of your hand. I miss all the words of encouragement that you gave me, trying to make my life easier.

My soul, my soul is on fire, I cannot survive without you. And without our baby, that decided to go to you. Maybe you already met him or her? I am presuming. I am guessing. I am begging. I am hoping. Wherever you are, I want to follow you. Whatever you want to do, I will do it with you. In that other place where you two are.

I am praying for the three of us.

Yours until forever,

Masha

Healing Time

"God put the Moon in the sky to remind us that our darkest moments lead to our brightest."

Lynne Ewing

In the time of the Balsamic Moon, I made my decision. I wanted to heal. To strip off all my anxiety and depression away. The time for sleep and rest before the New Moon, I dedicated myself to prayers and resolutions. I wanted to be the best version of myself.

I returned to LA and stayed in my family home. I was working with Luca very intensely, with energy healers as well; I had tons of homework to do by myself. I was diving into books, astrology sessions, crystal lessons, tarot readings… And I was very consistent with the time that I was spending on working on myself. I wanted to balance out my spiritual and practical sides.

That was the most powerful moment of my life so far. When I knew that I didn't have to tolerate other people's actions just for the sake of it. I would speak my truth and love myself, unconditionally.

As I was setting my feet in the ocean, looking at the horizon, there were three paths that I could take. Left, towards Francesco, whom I still loved deeply. Forever waiting to join him in Heaven, or wherever he is. Right, to Luca and all my angel helpers, who would love me sincerely and who would support me and help as much as they can. Or I could take a deep breath, taking in both sides, left and right together, and turn away from the water, walking down the sandy path towards the unknown. A new me, a new life.

I took that deep breath. Closed my eyes. Left, right… Or… The Unknown?

* * *

Luca was driving a red Porsche; he had a lot of money. He was born in a family of very successful lawyers and doctors. He was one of the more expensive and exclusive psychiatrists, so money was a normal thing for him to have. And give. He was a giver.

My father knew his father, so we were family friends, and patients. Especially my mother. That is why I initially never wanted to be his patient. Often I imagined being his friend; and being in the circle of cool people and celebrities that he knew. Life had other plans. I became his *patient*. He was careful and smart, a gentle doctor.

Talking about Mauricio was not easy, so I kind of just shortened that story to the basics, with the conclusion that I do not have a stable self-esteem nor self-compassion. But after losing Franco, I needed more. I needed to talk more. And Luca was one of the rare doctors in California that was offering medication treatment and therapeutic talk, all at once.

When my healing process started, I knew that Luca would be very persistent. He would try to help me at any cost. Or better to say, to make me heal myself. He believed that anyone could heal themselves if they want to.

I was used to being early to any appointment. Even in a zombie, depressed state, I was standing in front of his office, while he was parking his car.

"I'm so sorry, kiddo. Am I late?" He looked at his Rolex.

"No, Luca, I'm early. Old habits never die."

"Well, that one is a good one. As long as you don't wait too much. You yourself must respect your time."

Oh, great, session has begun before entering the office. I rolled my eyes. His office was like something out of a fairy-tale. Full of flowers, calming green and blue tones. It was such a nicely decorated place! Art on the walls. Crystals. And a very comfortable couch.

He made me a matcha tea, gave me a glass of water, and I set on the couch. Waiting for some miracle not to feel so anxious and go through this hour as painless as possible.

✶ ✶ ✶

"You are the artist of your life, Masha. You have the canvas, creativity, and all the passion that you need to be who you really are. It will never be as you imagined, if you do not pick up the brush and start painting."

"How do I do that? I feel lost, I feel drained. I am just going around the streets that surround my house and I feel like I am a zombie. Living dead. Whatever. Something, but not human. I lost the desire to smile. Not just the desire, I'm sure that if you asked me to smile now, I physically could not."

"I want you to trust me. I want us to build a trustworthy relationship, it has been a while since we had a session in person, living in the same time zone. I want to help you. You are going to be just fine. I promise you that."

I looked into his eyes, full of compassion. Even if I doubt that I will feel better, his eyes were convincing me to try. And Luca is good at what he does, and he knows me well.

At the first session, I did not get any prescriptions. We started the healing process without medication since the last one was not working, it was making me worse. Luca told me that he wanted to see how we progress through conversations and then he will decide on therapy. He was pretty sure of himself as a psychiatrist. And I wanted to believe in something, in someone. So, I decided to believe in Luca.

The next few sessions were torture. I was sitting or lying down for an hour; I was silent, he was silent and that was it. *Torture!* The atmosphere sometimes was worse than with Mauricio. It took me a few more sessions to start to talk…

✳ ✳ ✳

"Did I ever tell you about my teachers, my schoolmates, and what was happening with them?"

"No. What's the story there?"

"Well, I know that a lot of kids get bullied during school, but I remember coming home to my mother already on the brink of madness, locking myself into my room and thinking, *why. Why do I need to exist?* Bottom line, the girls in my class, for whatever reason, convinced the whole class not to speak with me. That day we had history first period, and I entered classroom just before the teacher. When I entered, the whole class looked at me and then turned the heads away from me. I was sitting with the girl who was the organizer of everything, of the whole "avoid Masha" scenario, so when I sat beside her, she got up and went to sit somewhere else. I did not shed a single tear.

During the class, I got a note from someone saying, "I am so sorry, Jenny told us not to talk to you, and she was pretty scary. I don't have anything against you." My tears started after I closed the door of my room. Cold mother, no friends. Father that I loved but was not present all too much, weird half-sister… I needed to go far, far away… I guess that was one of the events that started to screw me up."

Luca was listening to my story and making his notes.

"This is progress, Masha. We have a beginning and you are opening. I am really glad." I looked at him, and yes, it was obvious that he was satisfied.

And I felt that I can breathe just a little bit deeper.

* * *

I was driving back home the next day from the girl's night. I hadn't drunk since I was driving, and I was on several medications that Luca decided we should start 'testing'. So, I was not daring to drink any alcohol. Which made me distant, not funny, and I just wanted to go home and let them dance and have fun. My medications made me numb and tired, and I couldn't function after 10 pm. A couple of hours into the gathering, I said *bye,* if they even noticed that, and left.

In the car, on the radio, there was the song, *that* song, "Alone," and I felt that panic is building in my body. I pulled over and started to weep, I was sobbing, I was shaking. All I could see was Franco's dead body in front of me. I wished to hug him again. To run my fingers through his hair that was shining in the Sun.

"Why you, Franco? You were so happy. You wanted to be the father of our child. You were smiling, you were looking forward to the future. Why? You were so in love. *We* were so in love."

But no answer was coming back to me.

* * *

"Masha, I think it is time to start talking about Mauricio or Francesco."

"I'm not ready. We can talk about my friends; I don't know how to handle the current situation…"

"No. It's time."

I took a deep sigh. Talking about them would just remind me of all my bad decisions and bad luck, and I really didn't want to remember. I wanted to go forward. Wake up, put my clothes on, take a pill, put make-up on, smile, and go by my day. I did not want to talk about my tears and nightmares.

"I can talk about Mauricio. Well, there was that day…" I started.

"Yes, go on."

"I was in the supermarket, and I bought fish that I had chosen among all the fish in the supermarket fish aquarium. It seemed cruel and disgusting. I would never, ever do that again.

But that day, I remembered that Mauricio told me he really likes that specific species and they had it in the store. I had to buy it for him. I googled how to prepare it and I bought all the ingredients. That was my first time doing something like that. Cutting the fish, taking out the intestines, spicing it. I needed a lot of beer to not think about what I was doing. But with all that effort, I was still new to cooking, and the fish got a bit burned on the stove. Really not much, just a bit. Someone would say, it would give a special taste.

Oh, did I mention that I bought it with all the money that I had until the end of the month? It was an expensive fish. With the dinner ready and nice music playing, I was waiting for Mauricio to come back from work so we can eat together. I don't t know whom he was working with that night… Ah… When he came home, he looked at the slightly burned fish, lit a cigarette, and started to laugh at me, pointing to the fish. 'You burned it, ha! You are a horrible cook!' He said. I was just standing there frozen, not able to react. I wanted to cry, to scream at him, to say *why are you doing this*. But I just looked into his eyes and said, 'please, sit, you need to eat.'

You wanted to hear about Mauricio. Well, that's him. High on something and horrible. Beautiful and smart. And me, young and stupid."

"You needed that kind of experience to know who you are, and what you want or do not want. I am sorry that you had to go through that experience though. No one should be treated like that."

"I know now. I was obsessed with him. And with the desire to be his, I was that insecure. When he left me, I knew it was for the best, even though I was falling apart. I knew that we didn't have a future. I guess he did me a favour."

"Absolutely! He pushed you away himself knowing deep down that you two wouldn't work out. I believe that. I give him a bit credit for that."

"Well, later he married the girl that he was cheating on me with, so I guess they are both happy…"

Luca just looked at me. Slowly rubbing his temples. "Hard, hard life. Knowing everything about your family,

I am trying to be objective, but when I think about it all together, you had a really hard road."

"I guess so. But still, I turned out good, right?" I smiled.

He gave me a brief smile, but he became serious again.

"And then Francesco… I still see you in that prison cell, completely broken."

"Please, not today." I started to cry. Luca gave me a tissue box.

* * *

Next time when I saw Luca, I was sobbing in my palms, shaking, standing beside the window of his office. He got closer to me and pulled me into a hug. My head was still in my hands but I could rest it on his shoulder. He was silent and he was hugging me, brushing my hair, trying to calm me down. No words. Just one strong hug. It took me a while to calm down and continue talking.

"Francesco had beautiful eyes, a bright smile and amazing voice that went perfect with his guitar. I was thinking about his eyes all the way home, where he would wait for me. He was the center of my world. Nothing else mattered. I was running home every day, as soon as I could, just to be close to him. To watch his movements of the paintbrush. To look at his eyebrows furrow when he was thinking about his lines on the canvas."

"You were lucky you met Francesco. Someone who did not judge you, who supported what you did, who was also collecting all the pieces from your broken heart that were left after Mauricio. I don't think that you lost him. Everything is energy and energy cannot be destroyed, it just gets transformed. He's with you, in some shape or form. The Universe got you together and the Universe is still fighting for you to stay together, binding your energies. That does not mean that you will never be independent or will never love again. But when you have a love as big as you two had, it stays with you forever. That's why you are fine; you didn't lose Francesco."

I was listening to Luca's words of comfort and truth.

"You should not hurry with healing though. Everyone, including you, thinks that you have to heal quickly, that you need to know your next steps as soon as possible. But you don't. You can heal slowly, at your own pace and in your own time. Be gentle with yourself, Masha. *Love yourself.* We will need to work on that. Anyone who would come into your life now would need to respect and understand that you are taking care of yourself and working on healing properly. And while you do that, they will bring you coffee in the morning and tea in the evening and hug you to show you they care. That is why it is very important to choose the next man as someone who will love you tenderly and who will make you happy, additionally to the things that you do for yourself to make you happy. You *need* to be intentional. Fight for your smiles, always. Always.

And you will heal; never doubt that. You will. How many times in your life have you fallen? How many times have you thought you would never recover? But you did! So, you will recover from this too. I promise you. You are so strong. Not even the heaviest moments, when you lost faith in education or God, as you remember, stood a chance against your strength. That is where your hope is! Hope is in you! I respect you so much for believing in love in this world that is so obsessed with lust. You are a rare kind, Mashinka. You believe in magic and that is your pure soul that just wants to love and be loved. It is okay to have a soul that still trusts and has hope that good exists.

Do not judge yourself, I say again. And never stop believing that there is love so nourishing and deep that you will never need a pill or me. Never lose hope. And in this process, the hardest lesson will be to learn that you do not need closure, it does not serve you. With closure we think it will be easier to continue and move on, but no, we just put a bandage on and hope that the person is coming back to us. Sometimes closure is not beneficial. Because the person is not coming back, and we still need to heal from that. And closure is just giving us false hope that the end is not so near after all and that there is a chance… There is a possibility… *Maybe he still loves me, or maybe I imagined that he is dead, he is just getting better.* No, you do not need closure. Choose to mend you heart and choose to heal it."

Luca was holding my head in his hands and looking into my eyes. In that moment, I felt at peace, knowing that someone believes that I will be fine.

The Five-Year-Old Masha That Believed In Fairy Tales

"The miracle of grace is that you can give what you have never gotten."

Untamed by Glennon Doyle

The period of grief and healing was hard. Harder than what I expected it to be. I realized that for the most part of my life I didn't know who I was or what I wanted from my life. I was choosing my next steps without thinking, but subconsciously taking the same ones as before, each one of them one step closer to disaster. Yet, I was expecting different outcomes. The typical definition of madness. Until there were no more tears in me. Until I could no longer recognize myself in the mirror.

Through my self-improvement and past trauma work, I have learned, in baby steps, that I live only once and that every decision matters. If I wanted to have a good life, I need to work for it. The good job, the amazing husband, the perfect house, or any other thing that we want, it comes with dedication and persistence. Yes, if someone would look from the outside into the life of some 'perfect family' it would look like things are just coming so easy to them. But that's not true. In order for things to come easy into anyone's life, several things should be done; know yourself, love yourself, set boundaries, work for it and take action immediately when you see the opportunity to do so.

Luca and I worked for months on my brain health and mental health, trying to improve how much I know myself, how I organize my thoughts, my wishes and desires into precise actions that should be taken. Some of the work kept me awake at night, because I was trying to figure out how to proceed, and I wanted to be ready for my new life to start. The more I was learning about myself, the more difficult it became to keep some people in my life, and I had to learn that that will continue happening as long as

I am changing my choices and behaviours. I was making space in my life for the fresh and new.

It was time to finally feel better. I started to realize that it was time for a more authentic life. It was finally time to be the real me. All the events in my life that led me to this self-work, brought me to it with one purpose. I needed to learn to be my true self, no matter how hard that was. It was time to be me.

I found a nice condo near the beach, so I could have my morning walks. My feet touching the sand, feeling grounded and awaken by the ocean lapping against my calves. I started to apply for jobs in academia, even though, I thought that I was done with it. The love that I had for teaching resurfaced, and very soon that same love attracted several interviews for Assistant Professor or a lecturer positions. All of it happened so quickly, condo and interviews. I was purposefully taking time to stop, take a breath and soak everything in, every experience, to be aware and mindful about it.

By now, I had also learned that life is a mixture of very hard days and some unexpected, triggering moments. And even though I knew that, I decided to keep and protect one innocent part of me. The part of me that still believed in fairy tales, that in order to get to the happy ending you still have to face a few more obstacles. That imprint was still in me, I haven't worked on it. My inner child wanted to be kept in the safe space of finding the prince who will save her. I felt that. And I did not want to take that from five-year-old Masha. She has already lost enough. Purposefully, I kept that from Luca during our sessions, to protect the dreamy eyes of hers from the reality. I knew that it would not be smart for the grown part of me, because it would be triggered and who knows how it would manifest in this reality.

So, when I faced the first obstacles, I was again a young version of me, scared and insecure. I stopped my sessions with Luca, who was so confused, he could not understand why that sudden change. Since everything was going so well. I was not in the mood to explain myself to him, feeling like a failure, who after months of work, feels again bad, even worse than before.

It turned out that initial 'luck' to get some interviews, turned into a series of emails saying–no. Searching for a job did not go so well at the end. Interviews were a disaster, and I would be so angry at the world. *Why did I study so much all my life? To be nothing at the end?* I was waking up in the morning with a familiar feeling–depression was kicking in. Stronger than ever. I was applying to so many positions and nothing was coming from it. So many years of studying. Blood, sweat and tears for what?

At the same time, Luca was being blindsided by me and didn't know what to do. He suggested that I might try to date again, for the purpose of exposure and getting my self-esteem back. That would help my insecurity during job search. As much as I thought that I was ready to go into a relationship, I was not in the mood to do anything. I was especially not in the mood of kissing someone and faking a smile. I was still in pain, and being ready to live life as the real me was just not ready yet.

I was in my 30s with no job, no place to live as an independent person. Meaning that I had not bought any property as I thought I would at my age. I certainly didn't need a relationship with any random guy that I met on an app. So, even if my inner child was falsely thinking that we could be safe while a new person was in our life, taking the problems away; it is just that, an attempt of five-year-old Masha to take over my mind and my thoughts. She still believes that the prince is coming. One night, I decided that I had to talk with that inner child of mine and explain that not all fairy tales are becoming true. I tried my best not to be too harsh with her. Then I could start thinking as an adult, reducing the tantrums to a minimum. *My life is my responsibility and there is no man who can save me from myself. That is not how this works.*

Luca being a shoulder to cry on for so long, even that wasn't appealing to me anymore. I knew that I had to pull myself from the ditch. On my own. To solve one problem at the time. There was no time for a breakdown or giving up. This was the time to show my persistence and my strength and do all I can to get my life out from the chains of circumstances.

That reminded me of my childhood again, where in order to be or get anything, I had to do it myself. There was no one whom I could ask to explain to me how things are done. Nannies were barely speaking English, my Spanish was not so good at the time, and my parents were just… Not available. Not for each other, not for me. So, I needed to learn to be tough, to fight, to educate myself, to fly on my own.

* * *

After months of going back into self-work on my own, and finding my energy balance, *again*, I woke up one morning with a sense of calm and peace. I suddenly felt like everything would be okay. That brought a smile to my face. I got up and opened the curtains to let the sunshine come in. With the open window to allow a warm breeze to cuddle my face and rays on my skin, I meditated for as long as I felt comfortable sitting on the floor. My phone was in another room until I was done with my morning routine, that was my new rule. So, when I was ready to start my workday, meaning to start writing new applications for job positions, I saw an email from the University of California. The wave of optimism from the early morning was still in me, but now I was feeling anxious and scared. Until I've seen those long awaited and so much wanted words, "We are inviting you for an interview." I released a sigh of relief. *Not everything is lost just yet*, I thought.

Just like that, finally I got one interview, and it went well, and I got the position at one of the most prestigious universities as a full-time lecturer. I would be teaching students. I would be influencing their minds. *I will make them fall in love with science and nature,* was my thought every morning since I got the position.

I was mentally and physically ready for these next steps. I worked hard for them. I had changed so much in order to overcome my limitations. I knew I deserved this.

In the weeks to come, I was shopping for more professional looking clothes, and I had a big party with some old friends that stayed in my life, and with some new people that I met during my healing process; they became a part of my amazing, supportive crew.

* * *

My first day at UCLA as a lecturer, I was flying! I was happy and overwhelmed. I wanted to talk with every student separately, which was impossible. But I was trying to show them that I was there for them, and for their future. I did not want to take breaks. I just wanted to savour the feeling of being able to transfer knowledge to the younger generations and have a positive influence on their lives.

The dean invited me for lunch while introducing me to the staff that morning in the coffee room. I was so overwhelmed with my feelings that I almost missed it! At one o'clock I managed to run to the cafeteria where most of the staff came for lunch, and I spotted the dean talking with some other people. *Good, I am kind of on time.* I straightened my skirt and shirt, pulled my hair away from my face and approached the group.

"Ah, Masha, there you are!" His face was lit by his smile. "Everyone, this is our new colleague, Masha. She is joining us as a Neuroscience lecturer. Today is her first day. Masha, these are your new colleagues. You can ask them if you have any questions about anything regarding the campus, students, research. Anything really. They have been working here for some time now."

"Hello, it's a pleasure to meet you all." I said, as secure as possible. Then each of them started to introduce themselves.

"Hi, I am Sarah, professor of Biophysics. Nice to see another female here, finally! Anything you need, I am here!" Said the blonde woman with a ponytail and a genuine smile.

"I am Mark, Molecular dynamics freak. But I am not going to chase you too much to tell you about my experiments, I promise."

"Yeah, right, that's exactly what you'll do!" Sarah replied.

The last person was looking on his phone and typing fast. It looked like he didn't want to be bothered, so I very silently said 'Hi' to him, satisfied not to talk any further. But he looked up, straight into my eyes, and reached his hand towards me for a shake. As soon as he looked at me, I recognized him.

"Hello. I'm Adam."

"Hi, Adam. It is an honour to meet you! I've read so many of your papers. Your research is breath-taking!"

I stopped myself there, so that I quit sounding like a teenager meeting her favorite actor. He looked into my eyes, and I felt like I was glued to the spot. All my organs dropped down into the Earth. His face expressed something like a smile, like he was content with the hypnosis that just occurred. Then he returned to typing on his phone.

While in Rome, I read so many of his papers and at some point, I wondered how it would be to work for him. But that was a brief wish, before everything else happened in my life. Now that I am standing in front of him, I feel like this is exactly the place where I should be. Maybe everything in my life was leading me to this exact moment, where Adam Reeve Moore, MD, PhD is my colleague! I felt imposter syndrome slowly tapping on my door, but I did not open. *There is no time to feel small, Masha.*

"Well, I am hungry, let's go to eat!" The dean started to rush us into the cafeteria.

The five of us spent lunch chatting about different types of students, their interest in science and mostly listening to Sarah's advices for me. It was such a relief to be in an environment where I was feeling like myself again.

Where I was allowed to be myself again. I made jokes, I was smiling, they were interested in my experience I had obtained in the laboratory in Rome. And I recalled the memories about my experiments there, only. I blocked anything else that was waiting to surface.

Adam was the only one that was restraining himself from the talk, which was not a big surprise for me. He was a big shot in his field, I certainly admired his work. I did want to know more about him, though. There was an energy coming from him that screamed mystery, danger, genius. Everything that was always super attractive to me. My intuition was back after months of healing and I could sense people again, their core and their intentions. And Adam was giving out the vibration of loneliness, brilliance, and passion. With all of that, I definitely wanted to know more about him!

I remembered some articles that I read while in Rome about his personal life; divorce, kids, and complicated settlements. Adam was not only the most brilliant neurosurgeon, but he was also a son of a media mogul, and he was involved in relationships with so many famous ladies. It was not possible not to see those articles side-by-side with his research related ones, blinking and asking for your attention. Curiosity and a childish mood possessed me that day; and the look in his eyes when we met, made me lose control over my tongue.

"So, Adam, are you still active in rock climbing? Do you teach your kids to climb as well?" As soon as I said it, I felt the looks of everyone on me. *Why would I ask such a personal question on day one?* Suddenly, my enthusiasm felt so wrong! Adam's head rose from the phone, and he looked into my eyes. So deep that I felt chills from my head to my toes.

"How do you know those things?" He asked, leaning forward, deepening the look, which was now also sparkling.

"Well… You know… It was my job to read about your work, so that information came my way too." I said, my mouth going completely dry.

Adam stopped staring into my soul, and I could take a breath again. Everyone else seemed not to be interested in any more unnecessary questions, or they just simply wanted to save me from myself. Either way they looked ready to leave the table.

"Back to work!" Sarah exclaimed as happy as possible.

"Thank you all for joining me for lunch today. Masha, good luck again and my door is always open if you need me." The dean shook my hand.

"Thank you very much." I smiled.

Everyone hugged me and left, only Adam and I seemed to go to the same building. Which made sense, he was, technically speaking, my boss, as the head of the Neuroscience Department. The way to the building was silent and I was practically running to catch up to him. When we entered the building, I already had my speech ready to apologize for my question earlier, when Adam stopped.

"I am heading to the lab, so I will go right here. I assume you turn left." He stated.

"I think so, that is the only way I know for now." I answered.

"See you around. And welcome." We shook hands and he turned heading his way.

I started to walk towards my classroom, but I made a stop into my office. I closed the door and leaned on it. My whole body was vibrating intensely. Something felt so very familiar and so dangerous at the same time. I've felt like this already a couple of times before in my life, and it never ended good. This time, it already feels much more intense. *You have changed. You are not the same person as you were a year ago. Nothing has to be the same. You are overthinking and letting yourself to fall into the traps of your mind. You are fine. All is fine.* I told myself in order to calm down. *You will be fine.* I took a deep breath and continued my walk towards the lecture room.

✶ ✶ ✶

My past, all the experience that I've gathered through my relationships, showed me exactly who I am at that stage of my life. I was developing through each heartache. Sometimes, it hurt so much that I thought I couldn't handle it. But no matter how hard the situation was, I did survive. Mauricio, Francesco, each of them left unforgettable marks on my soul, but they did not destroy it. I grew from every fall, and I continued to walk forward. I rebuilt my life. Over and over again. On my own. No father, no sister, no brother. No motherly advice when I needed it. Completely alone. And each time, I was stronger than ever, with new scars to prove it. I won the battle and I do not plan to lose the war. I continued to believe in love. And after periods of grieving, I was ready to continue, to find love once again.

I also have learned that I cannot take this life for granted, because I am here for a specific reason. There is a mission for each and every person that walks on this planet. I do still search for mine, but I know that it exists. So, I want to continue to live, and laugh, and dance. And I want to love again. To this day...

* * *

Three months on the new job passed quickly, and I was so grateful for each day. I was waking up with a positive attitude already present, I was exercising, meditating, journaling, all before I would get ready for work. I started to change my wardrobe, I wanted to be more feminine, gentler, more me. I was celebrating small wins, like occasionally feeling like I am finally alive again.

Flying on that high vibration, made me a magnet for people who were more positive and happier. That was the law of attraction! The more you notice something, the more of the same you will attract in your life. So, I was paying attention to the good mood I was starting my day with. Dancing while brushing teeth and smiling to myself in the mirror. Telling myself, *you've got this girl!*

I was surrounded with immaculate students, great colleagues, and I felt so much more secure in myself, some self-love was noticeable. I had a few sessions with Luca again, but those were mainly filled with him being amazed how well I was doing. And convincing me to start dating again. He thought that I was finally ready. It was noticeable that men were more attracted to me those days. How predictable, right? As soon as I was finally feeling good with being by myself, men were all over me, paying for coffees, sending DMs on social media. Quite often, I would get a comment or a note from my female colleagues or girlfriends that someone asked about me or if they could introduce me to someone.

Waking up my femininity and working on myself to raise my vibration worked like a charm. However, I was not sure if I was ready to get involved, not just yet. It felt great to flirt and to be noticed, but the risk of opening my heart was too high. Yes, I have learned a lot through past relationships, like that I should be careful whom I trust. Yes, it is nice to have someone in your life, but be careful. Yes, eventually I wanted to be married and have children, but I needed to let myself be found by the man who will deserve me and take care of me. Now that I am writing this–the way I was thinking back then, and knowing what happened next, I feel foolish! You want to know why? Because I was a perfect case of, *Destiny is laughing at your plans.* As soon as I wanted to wait and be on my own and enjoy for a moment, the whirlpool of events led me to the recognition of my inner, most secret self.

Addicted To The Thing Called Love

"The lights are on, but you're not home
Your will is not your own
Your heart sweats, your teeth grind
Another kiss and you'll be mine."

Addicted to love by Robert Palmer

Somewhere I've read that in order for your life to flourish, you need to learn to be self-sufficient. I took it very seriously to start living by this statement. I had my job, I had my friends, I had uninterrupted 'me time'. I was healthy and working on my body and mind every day.

Luca was still trying to convince me that I was ready to date other people, and now that thought was in my head non-stop. *It could be nice to have some mature man beside me.* Briefly the thought would cross my mind while I was pouring coffee in the morning. I would shake my head and the thought would go away. Thankfully.

Those days, I was spending much more time working on the new lectures that would come in the next semester, since it was spring break. Long office hours were noticed by my head of the department, Dr. Moore. If we would meet in the kitchen of the department building, he would throw some comments in my direction like– 'Another long night, Masha?'. Or if I would yawn– 'Sleeping exist for a reason'. Sometimes I would laugh at his jokes, but there were times I would like just to be left at peace. I didn't feel comfortable being mocked by him, especially when I had so many comments to throw into his direction but I had to refrain as he was my superior.

When was it considered a bad thing staying late at work, or did I miss that memo while being in Europe? I started to avoid him, and to leave some work for home, so that I was not noticed too late in my office. As ridiculous as that sounds, I thought it would bring me some kind of peace of mind. But, after a couple of days, I noticed that

I actually *miss* his comments. I *wanted* to be noticed by him… *Getting into old patterns? Intellectuals with big egos?* I was telling myself, when my self-compassion leaves me just for a split second.

* * *

I'm in a big, dark, study room. One wall is a projection point for his presentations. The wall across is a dedicated board for writing, scribbles, ideas, and sketches. Whatever crosses his mind. The third wall is covered by shelfs and tons of books. The fourth has a huge door, and a small section of wall where a sofa sits with a small coffee table and two chairs on the opposite side of the sofa.

He is sitting in his office chair, and I am on the opposite side of the desk. His eyes are locked on mine. He is taking me in. Will I make a sudden movement? Will I smile? Or will I cry? Will I ask why I am in his office? And I want to ask many questions, but I do not want to give him the pleasure of winning this game of silence. I am provoking him. I want him to make the first move. Even though, my whole body is shaking, and I am scared. So scared. Not of him, but of the fact that I know deep down inside of me that

I am not that strong. I know there is something that can't be explained that is filling the space between us. I am in awe. In awe of the strength of it, in awe of the beauty of the power that it is providing. In awe of its power to heal me, from my past, present, and future.

Then he breaks the silence. "You know, life gets so complicated sometimes. I'm happy that at least with you I don't have to pretend and fake it. You turn me on. And I need you. And you know it." He is approaching me, taking me on his desk and making me moan. It is all happening so quickly. I am pulling him deeper inside of me. I want us to be one.

I woke up. My pillow was drenched in sweat. My heartbeat strong. Did I really just have a dream about Adam and me?

* * *

When I was around ten years old, I made a pact with myself. I would only be married, or continue a relationship if I was in love. Seeing my parents being distant and dysfunctional, sensing the differences and accumulating the weird energy every single day, my goal was not to have the same marriage story. Then there were all the fairy tales that have promised a happy ending when you find your one true love. So, my wish was to have only true love in my life, and not settle for anything less. That led to many disappointments, and men that were not good for me. I was realizing how oblivious I was to date them. Then there was a tragedy just when I thought I met my prince charming. Logically, I feared another heartbreak. Emotionally, I was hoping that Luca was right and there are men out there, who are good and will be ready to love.

However, it was ridiculous, outrageous, horrible, to even think that the potential person could be Adam! After I dreamed about him, the next few weeks were filled with my cheeks getting red anytime he would say hello to me. When I hear his voice in the hallway I try to avoid eye contact. I wouldn't go to observe his surgeries, which was my favorite teaching moment but now it was a nightmare because I was only focusing on his arms, or shape of his body.

I wanted to talk with Luca about it, hoping that he will put some sense in me, something like, "Hello! He is your superior! You need a better life, and not self-sabotage your entire career!" But I didn't tell Luca. I did not tell anyone what was brewing inside of me. Especially not when, out of the blue, Adam came to my office, and invited me to dinner.

"We could get to know each other a bit better." That was his excuse.

"It would be good to know *you* a bit better." Was mine.

* * *

I met Adam at the restaurant of the Hilton hotel. The pianist was playing "Clair de Lune" by Debussy. Adam was sitting in a corner table, dressed in a white shirt, holding a glass of red wine, completely emerged into the melody. When I approached the table, his face changed, he smiled like he was genuinely happy to see me. I haven't seen that look in anyone's eyes for so long. And just like that, the sensations of safety and security washed away any fear that I had before meeting him.

He pulled the chair for me and poured me some wine.

"Merlot is fine?"

"Yes, it is, thank you."

"I am glad that you came. I wasn't sure if you would." He confessed.

"Why is that?" I asked.

"You're a tough cookie. Sometimes I don't know what you are thinking. And lately you are not the most talkative people on campus." He smirked and his eye twitched. He briefly looked at the pianist to take some more of the music in. "You are mysterious, Masha. In so many ways. That's why I wanted to meet you and get to know you better."

He was giving me that same, dark, sparkly look that he had the first time when we met.

"Being mysterious is my thing, Adam. If you want to be my colleague, you should get used to that."

I was blushing, trying to present myself as secure. I was anything but. And I had a feeling that the darkness of the room didn't help in hiding the redness that was covering my face and at this point probably my neck too.

"Who says that I want to be just your colleague?" It was a firm, deep-voiced question that caught me off guard.

"I thought this was a friendly business dinner?" I said with a gentle laugh, after collecting my thoughts and all my energy, so as not to fall apart right there. *Is Adam flirting with me?* That was something that I certainly cannot allow to have at this point in my career. I already discussed that with myself. My brain was fighting hard with my soul in that moment. This man had so many famous actresses and models in his life, his ex-wife is one of them. He was one of the most successful neurosurgeons and scientists in the world, and one of my role models in research. Having a history like I have, a total fool for the intellectuals, he was the perfect guy to break my heart. The same heart that I spent years mending from guys like him, like Mauricio. *Red flag, red flag, red flag!* And yet, I was hypnotised by his look from the first moment, and I had the same feeling of familiarity that he had with me apparently. *At least I am more mature and aware of my feelings. I can handle myself much better now.* But my brain, soul, and heart were nowhere close of being coherent. My heart was beating so strong looking at Adam, and his casual smirk, while my soul was searching for those familiar moments from our past lives.

"No business tonight. I want to know you better. I just want to talk to you. Who are you, Masha Boki? Besides your research proposals and Roman experience…"

"I feel that I will become your 'solve the mystery' project?" And I immediately bit my tongue as soon as those words exited my mouth. *What is wrong with me, why am I talking like this to him? One half of the Merlot glass and I am an idiot!*

He smiled, looking like he was winning. I needed to take my power back. "Yes, that for sure. But beside that?"

"I am still searching for the answer to that myself. Probably that I'm a soul that wants to be awaken and live its purpose."

His eyes opened wider, and he took a deep breath.

"I think I just fell in love with your answer."

"Luckily it was only with my answer." I was flirting and I could not stop myself.

Both of us finished our wine in silence, listening to the enchanting music coming from the piano. Then Adam ordered another bottle. Conversation resumed and was going so smoothly that I almost couldn't recognize the Adam that I see at work, and this Adam, smiling, being silly and provocative. I liked this side of Adam. A lot.

At the end of the evening, he called his driver to pick him up and offered to drive me home. I did not refuse that; it was late and I was tipsy. Both of us in the back seat of a black SUV, each of us looking through our designated window. I was wondering what he was thinking. Then I felt his pinkie touching mine while our hands were resting on the car seat. My whole body was on fire. I didn't dare to look in his direction. I just let him catch my fingers in his hand. When we approached my building, the driver exited to open my door.

I moved my hand to unbuckle myself, and then my gaze caught with Adam's.

"Thank you for the dinner. It was really nice talking to you." I stumbled over my words.

Adam unbuckled himself and got closer to me. He took my face into his palms. His eyes were peering deep inside my soul. He kissed my cheeks one at a time, gently. When he paused in between, I started to shake. I wasn't sure what he would do next. But whatever it was, I was ready to receive it. I don't know whether it was the wine or his eyes, but I was under his spell. I was looking into his eyes, slightly opening my mouth, giving him the sign that it is okay. His breath was warm and sweet. He kissed my lower lip, then my upper lip. With a silent moan he slipped his tongue into my mouth, and I let him play with mine. I was suppressing my moan, but the longer the kiss, the harder it was to do that. I let myself make a sound, which made him even more passionate, and he was now pressing my body with his. I didn't notice the moment when the driver closed the door, but apparently at some point he did, and he was standing outside the car. When the kissing stopped, Adam hasn't opened his eyes yet and he was still holding my head with his hands.

"I hope this is not the last time. I hope this is just the beginning. Let me show you who I am beside what you have seen and heard about me." He whispered into my ear.

I closed my eyes, and there it was. The same feeling of familiarity from before. The feeling that we know each other from different lifetimes. It felt like we collected all the time from the beginning of the Universe in a bottle and we are pouring drop by drop. And tonight was maybe a drop too much.

"I hope so too. I hope so, too." Were the only words that I could have said at that moment. I could not force myself to open my eyes. I didn't want to open my eyes. Being held by Adam, in the back seat of his car, being kissed by him, no words to be spoken, was all I could wish for.

Was he the man that can handle everything that I have become and that I want to be?

✳ ✳ ✳

How many more times can I make the same mistake? I hadn't slept the whole night after the kiss. My usual sleeping pills did not work. I was looking at the ceiling, turning and tossing until dawn. I was trying to get up, changing the room, or just walking a bit through the apartment, then coming back to bed again. But no sleep was coming. As soon as I would close my eyes, there he was; Adam's face, his lips on mine, his hands on my cheeks. Another mistake with another unavailable man, in one way or the other. He is the chief, he is probably still officially married, and he's famous. And who am I? *Why, oh why, Masha, are you doing this to yourself over and over again? Self-destruction is not the way to live your life.*

I was not even sure how this happened, or when it started to happen, I don't know if I ever gave him any sign that I was interested in him. What made him invite me to dinner? Did he really like me? Was he even allowed to invite me to dinner like that? We're colleagues. Am I a victim here? Or is he the victim of my bad karma? This can't end well.

My brain wouldn't stop thinking. I was going into a downward spiral with all the experiences that I had in my life. My body was on fire, my body's temperature was rising, and when I checked, I definitely had a fever. It was morning already; sunshine was splashing on my exhausted body. I felt so sick, figuratively, and literally, and I was not sure if I was able to go to work that day. *Great. Already having sick days so early on the job.* My inner critic was working hard the whole night. But I did not want to allow myself to stay at home, manifesting my emotions into physical symptoms. I got up, showered, had some yogurt, and pulled together the best look I could in the state that I was in. *And off you go, girl. Own your mistakes with pride.*

When exiting my building, I saw the SUV that looked like the one that drove me last night. And the same driver was standing beside it. The window at the back seat pulled down, and Adam's face appeared.

"Good morning, chica. Cómo estás?" He said with a huge smile on his face. "I am barring two coffees, and one is for you. Want to share a ride with me to work?"

I was standing still as a statue for I don't know how long, in shock from the sight in front of me. Magnetically attracted, without words, I entered the car. The smell of Adam's cologne and coffee made me shiver.

"Thank you" I said reaching for the coffee, trying not to look into Adam's eyes. *What the hell is happening right now?*

* * *

That was the beginning of a very electric month. The events and the people going through my days were out of my control. My life seemed completely taken away from me. My mind and body had their own decisions, and did not want to submit to the reasonable part of me, that I believed was somewhere buried in me. I believed that the reasonable Masha was hidden in some specific corner of my brain, and I just needed to find her. All was chaos, chaos at the verge of destroying everything with the next step I take. And those steps were unpredictable, fast, and confusing. I could not recognize myself. With all the self-work done, someone would think that I would know better, decide better, about all the things in my life. But I was a completely different version of myself than expected.

Like there was something to be learned, understood, clearly telling me that I was still not demon-free. I was dark. I wanted dark. I wanted risky. I wanted dangerous. I was excited by it. Even though I should have feared it, I didn't. Fear did not exist that month for me. I did not know where this would lead me; if it leads anywhere at all but to self-destruction. And this time, a complete burnout of me. I would burn from the inside-out and become a pile of ash.

The feeling of magnetic attraction was all I was thinking about. Job, friends, people that are getting hurt by this behaviour, my dignity, that was not important. The only permanent surrender was to Adam's messages. Where he calls me to come. To specific addresses. Where we would meet. Where he would spend hours reading my mind and marking my desires that he wanted to fulfil. My days were spent waiting for his summoning. There was no other place I wanted to be. The hot spot was Adam himself. And his lips. His arms. His entire body.

He played my body with his tongue, like playing the violin strings. He used my neck to make me beg for more. *You are mine*, were the words carved on my thighs where he would bite them.

I did not care about fancy restaurants, presents, or trips that he was planning for us. I was addicted to him, and only him. I was agreeing and accepting anything, so that I can skip to the part of the evening when he would take me. The only talk I wanted to hear was his pillow talk. Even when he would talk science and kiss my arm, I was close to exploding. He was sensual. He was so good at making anything desirable. I swear, even him quoting his future paper, whispering it into my ear, made my body move under him, longing to be taken.

It was scary to think that this would be over. This period of pure passion. Adam attracted me with one look. And he made me his, contract signed in lust, in the deepest darkest night. *What if this ends quickly*? My anxiety asked me, when in the classroom full of knowledge-hungry students. They were my primary focus just until recently, before Adam's first kiss.

People were talking about us, assuming what was happening. Someone told me that I should report him if he was taking advantage of me as his employee. That made me so angry that I tossed my coffee into that person's face. I was suspended from work for a week, only because I did not have any prior behaviour problems.

I was losing myself. Voluntarily. To Adam.

* * *

One rainy night, while lying alone in my bed, somewhere between dreaming and being awake, Francesco came into my thoughts. That was his first visit after a very long time. And it confused me. Why was he here when I am so deep into someone else. Feelings of shame and guilt started to surface.

I was looking into his big, beautiful eyes and mine started to fill with tears. When he hugged me, I was already sobbing. His blue aura made a bubble, shielding both of us.

"I am sorry, I am so sorry." I barely managed to say.

"There is no need to be sorry." He kissed my wet cheek.

"Yes, there is. I am betraying you! I am sorry! And you're here! I am sorry, I'm sorry!" I couldn't stop crying.

"Shhhh, mi amore. Everything is all right. You're not doing anything wrong."

"Forgive me, please, forgive me."

"There is nothing to forgive, Masha." He gently moved my hair away from my face. He looked as radiant as I remember. As gentle as always. I missed him.

"I... I... You're here!"

"I will always be with you. Always."

I buried my head into his chest. He still smelled like fresh plums. That was the smell that I missed so much. For a long time, I was searching for anything that smells like that, perfume, cologne, anything that I could have to console me. There was nothing like that. But now he was here. I could nearly taste the smell; I could almost kiss the skin on his collarbone.

"Don't go away again, please. Don't leave me alone. I cannot… I am not myself without you. Please do not leave me." I begged, I cried, I was holding onto his shirt so tightly.

"If there is anything that I want, it is to be able to be beside you again. I want you to know that. I never wanted to leave you. The both of you."

My stomach was tying itself into knots, and I felt pain in my lower abdomen. I remembered the feeling of our child in me.

"Don't talk about that. It hurts."

"I'm sorry. The thing is, it will always hurt. To remember. At the same time, it will always feel like love. Because it was. It is. It will always be. Do not fight it; it is a part of your life. It made you into the woman that you are now."

"I am a mess," I cast down my eyes, so he doesn't see my disappointment in myself.

"You are transiting into a new life. That's messy. You are not the mess itself. And it is okay, to be scared, confused, lost. So, you can be found again. Masha, it is okay to be found by someone again."

"No! I will lose myself. I'm already starting to, and I will lose you!"

"You will never lose me. If you need me, you just need to close your eyes and think of me. And I am right beside you. But to lose a bit of yourself for someone, that is okay. That's what being in love means. You need to love again. To trust again. You are the most beautiful soul that I have ever known. You can give so much! Don't close yourself off. Promise me. Promise me that you will try. Promise me that you will let someone inside your heart again."

Francesco kissed my forehead and I felt lighter. Once again, I almost kissed his skin on the left collarbone. The blue light was fading, so I closed my eyes not to see him leave.

When I woke up, sweat had soaked my sheets and pillowcase. The Sun was beaming through the curtains. It was morning. I hugged the pillow beside me that was not wet and stayed in bed to bask in the feeling of the dream.

I did not know if I could ever love again or let someone love me. Giving my body to someone was not scary. But my heart was another thing. I wasn't sure that I could do it. But I need to try.

* * *

Later that morning, I did my best makeup and hairstyle that I could. I slip into my sky-blue midi dress and beige pumps with 2-inch heels. It was always important for me to look good for myself if I wanted to have courage to do or say something that is important to me. And at this specific moment, I needed to talk to Adam. To clarify what was going on with us. The dream of Francesco was still so fresh in my mind, and I needed to keep my promise. *I will try to open my heart again.*

I found Adam in his office, holding his head with both hands over his laptop, serious and barely moving. Since the office door was open and his administrator was not at her desk, I gently knocked on the door.

"Yes?" Adam said without raising his head or moving.

I cleared my throat, and quietly said, "Hi. I am sorry, I don't want to disturb you… If you're busy, I can come back later."

He looked up and his face lightened when he saw me. He smiled and stood up from his chair. The immediate change in his energy made me smile back. He closed the office door and approached me. He hugged me tightly and then gently kissed my lips.

"You look so beautiful!" Adam was scanning me from head to toe. "Is there any special occasion today?"

"Not really. Just feeling good in my skin."

"Oh, that's the thing that women say. That they do not dress for any man but for themselves, correct?"

"Something like that…"

"Well, your feel-good look influences the opposite sex very much." His eyes were getting darker and he was pulling me closer to him, until there was no free space between our bodies. He leaned in for another kiss, but I stopped him.

"Listen, can we talk shortly?"

His body straightened and he gave me freedom to pull myself from the embrace. He gestured to the chair where I can sit and he settled in his chair across the desk and looked at me, waiting for what I was going to say.

"I want to be brief and on the point," I started. "This past month was the craziest month of my life. I've never felt like this, completely out of control. I am used to having order in my life. Or at least be able to prepare myself for the things to come, by approximately knowing what is going to happen. Being able to sense the next steps is my thing. Until life gave me some hard lessons." I started to realize that I was going too far with this, so I made a break for a few seconds to collect my thoughts.

"Anyway, being careless and taking things for granted is not something that I want in my life anymore. It's not good for me. I want stability and security. I need to be stable and secure for other people too. In the past weeks, I was not.

Being suspended, not thinking about the consequences, not asking questions, and just surrendering to the temporary satisfaction… Well… We're not in the movies. This is real life. And I am not delusional to believe that I can take the place of any actress or model that wants to be in your life. Another thing is, you are not done with your divorce, and I don't want to cause anymore disturbance. Again, totally irresponsible behaviour from my side. And, on top of everything, we are colleagues as well. You're technically my boss. I don't want to be caught in a case of being called 'position hungry' or 'promotion mistress' or whatever else it might be."

At this point Adam was looking at me, all his facial muscles tight with tension. But he was not surprised by my words. Or at least he didn't show that he was.

"I do have feelings for you," I continued, "more than I want to admit. And all the craziness in my behaviour was due to the walls that I have built around my heart. It's easier to be careless and blame it on not thinking, rather than admitting that my walls of self-defence could be down, and I eventually could get heartbroken. Somehow, you managed to get into my heart. I do not know how or when, but you did. And I would be ready to put my walls down completely. For you. But... I need to know, to be certain, that you feel something too. I need some kind of security. We are on a dangerous, slippery slope and I need a proper partner to help me, *us*, pass it."

I let out a deep sigh. I was done with my speech. I felt like I just signed my resignation letter and broke up with him at the same time. When I managed to look up, Adam was looking very calm now. No tightness in his face, no weird expressions. He was just looking at me, collecting his thoughts.

"I appreciate that you came to me and told me how you feel." Then he took a longer break. "I want you to know that I think that you are a smart, intelligent, capable women. You have a type of scientific brain that I always wanted to find in someone. I respect you as a colleague and a scientist. If it means anything, you will have a place in my department as long as I am here. The suspension that happened was out of my control though, it was more of a security matter, as far as I know."

I wanted to interrupt there, and thank him for the words, but I was hoping that there was more to that. I did not want to conceal this conversation as–we had fun and now it is over. Suddenly, I started shaking, realizing that, *oh my God, I do have real feelings for this guy. And I want to hear that he has them too.* My heart started to beat faster. A panic attack was on its way. My palms were sweating, cold drops were going down my neck and back. There was no air in the room that I could breathe in. I jumped up from the chair.

"I am sorry. I need to go." That was all I could say and ran out from the office. In the closest restroom, I splashed my face with water and made my tears less distinguishable. *You made a fool of yourself again, Masha. Bravo!* When I managed to get to my office, I took my medication. Then I started with some breathing exercises to calm down. Soon, I started to feel better. I reached for my phone to check my schedule, so I could know when exactly my next class was. And there it was, a message from Adam.

"Before you decide that you don't want to see me again, or leave, you need to know something else as well. I have feelings for you too. Best, Adam."

I silently whispered with my eyes closed, "Thank you."

* * *

The Sun was strong, the tiny breeze was warm. You could take a deep breath and feel the power of nature. Stepping into sand that burns your bare feet and cooling them with the ocean waves coming to greet you. So many people walking around, playing beach volleyball, kids running to get the best sand for the castle that they're building. I'm sitting on my towel, hugging my book, but my eyes are still focused on the blue ocean. Since I woke up, I am repeating Luca's words. "Let go of expectations. Remove focus from the specific thing, let the energy come back to you. Take care of yourself. Be compassionate with yourself."

Since the last meeting with Adam, I've retreated from socializing with people from work. I was going to the campus to give my lectures, and before and after that I was in my office, available only for my students. I didn't want to seem unpleasant to my colleagues, they have nothing to do with my decisions, so I had some friendly chatting if I met them in a coffee room or a hallway. But that was all. I did not go for drinks, or dinners. Officially, I was busy with organizing my life, focusing on my work, and writing my book that will be used as a study guide at the university. All of that was true, and still, it did not cover the main reason. I was not *ready* to see Adam. I didn't want to see him and be triggered to jump into his embrace and let everything else go to waste. My plan was simple. Out of sight–out of mind. No communication, no messages.

Emails that were coming from him were only general and sent to the whole department. Those made a knot in my stomach, when I would see the name of the sender, but soon the feeling would settle and I could breathe again. Focusing on my work was very beneficial. My wish always was to teach and be surrounded by young, smart minds, so I would lose myself into that. And the students were always eager to ask question, to think deeply, to ask for advice about studying or about career development. They made my work not feel like work at all. There was no day when I haven't felt gratitude to have this job and those souls around me.

Nights were hard. Even if I would continue working, there was a point where I would need to rest. But my thoughts were spiralling. *Does he ever think of me? If he really has feelings for me, why did he just let me go like this? Maybe he needed some kind of reply from my side, in order to reach out again?* I saw him once, a couple of months after my shut-down, he was coming down the stairs while I was entering the main building. He gave me a deep, dark, sparkly look, his trademark, and nodded with his head. I nodded back. I felt his energy being closed, locked. He closed himself too. A wave of cold air went through me, and chills reached every inch of my skin. *Maybe this is for the best. What did I expect to happen?* But I knew exactly what I wanted to happen.

I wanted to believe him and all the words he had told me before. I wanted to be swept away. But when it started to happen, I was scared, unsure. I wanted to hide in a dark corner of the room and not see anyone. I was scared to trust again, to see a new man as someone I can trust. I was scared of losing myself completely, *again*, and then getting hurt. *Again.* Especially knowing that he was loved by so many women. That made me hungry to feel safe and secure.

My work with Luca now involved much more self-compassion work. I needed to learn how to take care of myself and to learn how to love myself. I was so quickly captured in someone's romantic gestures in only the first few weeks, and Adam gave me a lot of reasons to be scared and careful. Because, who gives that much? Not a man who can have any woman in the world! *And he chooses me?* That happens in movies, yes, and is followed by complete dedication and submission in return! By not loving myself, I could not believe that anyone else could either.

My biggest scare happened when he did not ask for anything in return. He was genuinely in love with me, fast and deep. I remember being on the weekend getaway with my girlfriends and he would land with his helicopter on the beach close to us and come bearing gifts for all of us. Then he would take me into his arms and kiss me like he hadn't seen me in years, even though it had only been three days. He would tell me that he loves me in every Universe. My girlfriends liked him, but there was a dose of scepticism in them too. *Be careful,* was their advice. The obsession was real, so I knew that I wouldn't be careful, not while I was so close to him. And having angry outbursts at work did not help.

So, there I was, buried in work, into words, into possibilities and theories. Yet all of them lead me to the ones about Adam. I could not understand what Francesco wanted to tell me in my dream. If it was not about Adam, who was he talking about?

* * *

A ball of pink light was surrounding me. It gave me a sense of safety and security that I have not felt before. I was floating in the ball like I am weightless. Me and the pink ball could go wherever I turned my mind. There was a pit-stop made in a circus tent where I could fly in circles around the sandy stage in the middle of the tent. The next stop was a Turkish market where I was offered delicious fruits and met some people that made me join them for karaoke night. Like that was not enough, I found myself in a Lenny Kravitz music video, where I just had to look mysterious and not pay any attention to Lenny while he was on his knees, singing lines from his song directly to me. And then, there it was, a hotel room, clothes tossed on the floor. Adam kissing my back while pulling me closer to him so I can feel his excitement.

He whispered in my ear, so I could feel his warm breath. "I want to sweat with you, in your kisses, in your hugs. I want to make you crazy, so you beg for more while I touch you where nobody has touched you before, to make you tingle and suffer. I want to make love with you. I want to have you. I want to bite you, I want to have you now, right now. To chew on your neck. To lick your ear. I want you!" He placed me flat on the bed and kissed me. *"You are mine. You always were, and you will always be. You signed the contract. You gave your soul to me. It is done."* I screamed when he entered me, a mix *of pain and perfection. There was no way to escape. I am his. There is no other way.*

That realization made me wake up, I woke up so sick, that I could not breathe, my throat was swollen, my head was bursting, and everything was spinning. I did not know if I had the ability to even get up to go pee, but I had to try. I went to the bathroom, and there, on the floor, on my knees, I was begging God to keep me alive with every move I make. I loved living alone, but I really, really wanted to have someone with me at this moment. I was so ill that I could not imagine trying to get changed, and then make tea all by myself. And then I remembered my dream. With him. *If I could just call him to come to help me… No. I am alone in this. And why would I need any man ever, if I am alone when I need someone the most?* My anger started to rise, as was my fever. My body was once again fighting my mind, telling me to slow down, to take care of myself more, now by allowing me to catch the virus that was going around among the students as well. I felt that I have every right to be furious at life, destiny and especially Adam.

* * *

What becomes of the hopeless romantic whose heart has been broken so many times? Ice cube-like soul? Bitter soul? Angry soul? Well, me, Masha, resembled all of it at once. Luca and I had sessions sometimes twice a week at that point in time, but even he did not manage to make me less angry.

"You are a strong young woman Masha, but you do not need to beat up the next man you see on the street." He would say, with all the sincere compassion he had for me.

"Even if I wanted to, I'm not that good." I would huff in his direction.

Boxing classes became my new training routine, and I loved them. For that one hour, I would sweat all the emotions out of me. It felt so good to be in some kind of control. Maybe I did imagine using boxing moves on certain people, so what?

After four months on a very strict diet regiment, Adam-free ingredients only, I had thought that I was good now. One day I woke up, got ready for work, drove to the campus, gave my first two lectures, had lunch with colleagues and only when I was back for my afternoon lectures did I realize that I did not think about Adam once. Here is the thing. I always knew that I was living in my own definition of normal. My reactions are not necessarily the reaction you would usually get from other people. So, when the realization was made, I felt an excruciating amount of pain and disappointment. You should not forget someone like that. Other people would say, *no, that is exactly what you should experience; you had fun, but now you move on.* As I am not one of those rational people, that did not make sense to me. Everything that I have done in my life, was because I was following my heart, not only my intuition. I was going where love was pointing me to go. Even when everyone and everything around me was telling me that I was making a mistake.

Adam's eyes, that day when I saw them for the first time, his smile, the way he spoke my name, the way he wanted to take care of my wishes, was the reason why, when I realized that I hadn't thought of him, I felt guilty. *Ashamed.* What happened to the hopeless romantic who gets her heart broken so many times? The romantic feels lost and full of regret. The romantic realizes that what is in the heart, you can find only in the eyes of a true soulmate. Pure heaven.

I opened my email on the phone and typed a message to Adam. That is what the hopeless romantic does.

* * *

Adam did wait for a response from me, to not only continue where we stopped, but he did much more than that. He made it official. HR was involved, he wanted to be sure that there were no issues around our relationship. Yes, he called it a relationship. He told me, "I want to be in a relationship with you, Masha. I don't want to play around with you. You deserve to be the only one." His divorce was finalized a couple of days before I contacted him, so it was perfect timing. I just needed to tell myself that I was ready for this. That I am ready to believe in someone again. So, I was reminding myself to take deep breaths.

This time around, Adam was all-in. He was spoiling me even more with presents and weekend trips. And my favorite, notes around the house with messages–*I love you, my doll. Brainstorming balcony time!* Or, *meet me in the shower.* What I know is that if I wanted to go to space, he would call a guy and buy one rocket for my trip. Just like that. Yes, he was rich, according to Google. But he was also self-accomplished. He made his own money with his ideas in the industry. He liked to be a scientist, surgeon, doctor, and businessman.

He brought me to a villa, overlooking the ocean, where the whole upper floor looked like we were in a castle. Half-turned to glance at the ocean, we were drinking wine, eating caviar, oysters, but mainly we were kissing and laughing like teenagers.

"Let's dance, Masha." He asked for my hand and swirled me across the floor. I loved the song, *Someone like you*, and I was smiling. Ecstatic from all the surprise and happiness; the whole evening was romantic. Adam was fixating on my pupils with his smile, touching my waist, puling me closer and closer.

"In the mood for a selfie?"

I was laughing.

"Yes, that's what all the people do, not only my generation."

The ocean was in the background. My hand on his hip. He took my phone to take a picture, with a free hand he was holding the place below my waist. After taking the picture of us, he gave me a necklace. The sapphires blinding me from the sparkle.

"It looks so beautiful on you. You are giving it life. You are my life." He caught my face with both of his hands. His lips were kissing mine. I felt warmth in my stomach. He was making me tremble. And for the first time, clearly, he made me feel like I wanted something more with him. Could he be the one that I would spend the rest of my life with?

* * *

Some trips with Adam were spontaneous. One day, I was working on my lectures, and the next, we would be driving down some coastal road across the world. I was letting my hair down to be dried by the warm Mediterranean wind. I was singing and smiling and forgetting all my troubles. I would be looking into his eyes, blue as the sea. Filled with pure happiness. He was slowly but surely curing my spirit.

I started to open more and be honest about who I am truly, the independent girl, who travels the world, learns languages, and has big dreams. One who is not afraid of anything. Adam loved that about me, and he supported it. That distinct independence with a pinch of tenderness, female energy that seeks attention when it awakens. Yes, he loved that. And he was the same. He was traveling a lot, and he would lose himself in his work. He was the best surgeon at the Children's Hospital LA and an amazing scientist. And I loved that! I loved listening to his talks and scientific discussions. Seeing him studying before his tasks and thinking in front of the board, was very sexy.

With such a similarly functioning brain to mine, he knew how to support me in what I wanted to become. And I knew how to be a woman of a strong man. I found that in me, too.

* * *

At the end of the day, after everything that had happen in my life, I was still scared to enter a deep, emotional relationship. But so was he. His last one, was a five-year-long marriage. Even though the fear was there, the passion was stronger. And we had a desire to be with each other all the time.

I remember one night we went out with lots of colleagues after work, to just release the pressure of the week, and we drank a lot. Like, *a lot*. Even though everyone knew that we were together, we did not want to behave inappropriately.

Especially in front of the dean. But that evening, I could not stop looking at Adam, and he was following me with his gaze. We would find each other's eyes wherever we were in the room and just lock them. All the emotions floating between us. At some point one colleague wanted to take a picture and Adam was standing beside me, taking my waist and pulling me so easily towards him, I felt like a bird on his palm. After the picture was taken, he grabbed my butt and I gave him a warning look. He smiled. And winked. Later, at the parking lot, I ran into his hug and we both leaned our heads on each other's shoulder.

"I hope I can spend this kind of evening with you every day, little one."

"I hope so too. I hope so too." I barely manage to say it, my voice shaking with desire. He smiled at me, while my heart was pounding 150 beats per minute. I was deeply in love with him.

* * *

Adam was becoming a lion in his professional and personal life. I knew that it was not smart of me to not be able to control myself around him, but I could not help it. He would call me into his office, and I would close the door behind me. He would press me against the wall, kissing my neck slowly. Licking my collarbone. I would pull his hair and bring his head back to my face, looking into his eyes, kissing his upper lip. Faster and faster until I could not resist it and I would bite his lower lip. He sighed. His hands did not stay long on my breasts, he pulled my skirt up and put his hand in my panties. He felt how wet and warm I was. He pushed himself towards me and I felt his desire. He removed my underwear and moved me to the desk.

He was kissing every toe, my leg, every inch of it, and then pulled my long skirt completely up so I could see his eyes while he was pleasuring me. That was the first time that I could relax with any man while he was going down on me. And it was so seductive, I could not get enough of it. Adam was sighing and enjoying every sound coming out of me.

When I couldn't resist any longer, I stopped his mind-blowing performance, undressed him, and pulled him into me. We were perfect with each other. I lost track of place, time and space. We could be moving forever. Kissing each other at the same time. When my spine arched backwards, he was sighing louder.

Our pace was getting slower, we wanted to look each other in the eyes. The slow pace, the kisses, the energy, made us finish at the same time. Our bodies mixed. Our souls were truly happy. Our hearts were full.

We smiled. We cried. We kissed. We were in love.

∗ ∗ ∗

One day, I was coming back from my yoga class. I saw Adam on the balcony of his master bedroom, barefoot, in white shorts and a white linen shirt, looking at the ocean in a meditative state with his eyes open. That was when his great ideas would come. I looked at him, smiled, and went straight to take a bath. Sometime later, he would knock on the bathroom door and enter with two champagne glasses.

"What are we celebrating?" I asked.

"What do you think about going to Egypt? I need some of its energy. My brain craves desert and dust, and a land full of history." He said with passion in his eyes.

"Absolutely! I can write my lectures for the upcoming semester from anywhere and I've always wanted to see it." I was happy to travel with Adam. That meant luxury, exclusive sightseeing, and feeling everything at its maximum. "Cheers!"

"Cheers, my love." He said and then kissed me.

* * *

Late afternoon the very next day, we were already in Cairo. We made love as soon as we entered the room. So gentle, yet passionate and sensual. He was kissing my collarbones, a favorite spot of mine when it comes to Adam kissing my body. I never told him that, but I guess my moaning gave me away. After we finished, he placed me on the bed and covered us partially with the sheets. He was gently passing with his fingers down my arm, my hip, until my toes, and then kissed every toe. He leaned on his hand on his side to look at me, deep into my eyes.

"I don't ever want to lose you. You are my favorite person in the world! You are the only human that I can trust. I have never felt like this, and believe me, in my 50-something years of life, I have enough experience to know that."

"Oh, yeah? Want to tell me about the experiences?" I said without any actual desire to hear about all the models he's been with.

"Nothing interesting to say. None of them were you."

I smiled. He smiled. In those moments, I thought that we were really made to be together and that nothing could come between us.

After he fell asleep, I went to the balcony and looked at the pyramids and prayed for a sign, what to do. I knew the legend; *those who come to Egypt, will get the solution.* Couples either stay together or they part. There was something in the air in this country. There was history, murders, passion, blame, guilt, love, pain, happiness, hope. Adam brought me here, not knowing that I needed this. Or did he?

When I woke up in the morning, not feeling any jet-leg yet, Adam was not beside me. On his pillow there was a red rose and a note, *See you later. My most loved one!* Him and his busy schedule... I was wondering where he is now, thinking and doodling his ideas. However, I had everything what I needed to pamper myself the whole day. Butlers, maids, personnel that would bring me clothes that I want. I just had to move my finger in the right direction. Anyone could get used to this! And without guilt, after everything I have been through, and all the medications, tears, disappointments, therapy–I was convinced that I deserve this. I *should* be pampered. I *should* enjoy life. I *should* love myself more. And Adam loves me enough to understand that.

He does not cross the boundaries that I set regarding my past stories, and my future goals. He just wants me.

And still, he gives me the world anyway. And I accepted that contract. *He is my healer. He is the prince that I needed.* And where all of that would lead, I did not know. I did not want to know.

My day was perfect, filled with massage, manicure and pedicure, shopping, and I could not help it, so I visited one pyramid alone, without Adam. Then I had a long, nice, jasmine bath. When I emerged to the master bedroom, Adam, dressed in white, was standing at the balcony overlooking the desert. Rose petals on the balcony floor, he is singing *Endless love,* inviting me to join him for a dance, and I see the sapphire ring lying on the table. We kissed to seal my *Yes.*

* * *

I remembered Luca's words that I needed to stay open. My heart needed to heal, but it did not have to be closed. The more open it is, thus vulnerable and exposed, the better chances for me to heal faster. And there he was. Adam. Older, wiser, in love with me. I needed someone like Adam. To push me, to know me better than myself.

When he proposed, I knew I was not in a state to make rational decisions, to think with my head too. My heart was making the choice. I was allowing myself to be exposed and naked. There was no other option but to try to be. Did I have doubts? Yes. Adam was famous in more than one way. He was desired by so many. Rationally, I knew that he was a dangerous choice for me. So, I based my decision only on my heart. I said yes. And generally, I was happy with that choice.

The period from me saying *yes,* until the day in the church, passed so fast. I barely remember how I chose the wedding dress. I just know that I didn't have a budget. I enjoyed being spoiled with everything. Adam gave me his black card and I was on. I had a wedding planner, so it was easy. I could work at the University without taking time off. In three months, we pulled off the wedding of my dreams.

Dreaming With Eyes Wide Open

Change is the only thing that you should consider forgiving your partner. Maybe he or she really needed it. Have a talk. Probably it was for the best.

Did you ever consider that change can be a thing that crushes your heart? Not to mention the hearts of the people around you who would be affected by your change. However, change is the only thing that must happen for matters to progress. It is our only constant. Every few years, I had that flood of emotions inside of me, and I knew that no matter who was beside me or where I was, emotions would be so intense that I had to move on. From someone, from somewhere, from the old version of myself. I had that in me, that fire that burns everything, inside my soul, my whole life, just to make space for a newer, better version of it. And as much as I wanted love, I knew it would take a very strong man to be my man. That complete realization, after years of working on myself, made everything so clear. I'm the main reason why men in my life could not stick around or were the wrong choices for a long-lasting relationship.

Once I observed Adam performing a surgery, from the gallery of the O.R., at the Children's Hospital. He looked like a God. Tall, strong, in white, secure in what he was doing. I could not connect the Adam I had spent time with in Cairo or at home that first year of our marriage with the Adam I was looking at in the O.R., saving a child's life. There were so many women in the gallery that day, and questions started to line up in my head. How many of the doctors or nurses had he slept with in this hospital? That question had to come because many of them looked at me with the expression of jealousy.

I was not a typically jealous person, I did have my moments when I would feel that spark of *this person is mine*, but at this specific moment, I was just looking at my man saving a human life while listening to rock music. When the song *If God will send his Angels* started, he looked straight into my eyes, somehow, he knew exactly where I was in the gallery, and smiled. At least, the corners of his eyes lifted. I smiled back. God, I did love this man, in such a different way than any other man in my life. This was grown-up love. Calm and easy. Easy was the key. For at least that first year, when all the red flags looked pink to me.

* * *

I was sure about many things in my life. Or I thought I was. One of them was that I *should* be with Adam. That first year of our marriage, I was on cloud nine, all day, every day. Adam was behaving as a perfect husband. The one that you would really call a prince. He was that. He played the role so nicely, there was not a single doubt in my mind that our relationship would be anything but perfect.

I remember one day, or specifically, one night, when I felt so loved. Nothing extraordinary happened but it was an example of how my days looked like. After our honeymoon, I started to work again, went back to the auditorium giving lectures. As soon as the end of the working day would come closer, I wrote a message to Adam asking him where we should meet after work. I got a reply a couple of minutes later.

'How about somewhere in West Hollywood?'

I replied *yes*, and quickly afterwards I got the meeting point and time. It was the type of restaurant where you had to be someone of importance to get a table, especially so quickly. Time–6 pm. Everything with him felt right. It felt exciting, I felt like my true self. I was waiting for that feeling for so long. And here we are. At 6 pm. He was looking at me while I was entering the salon and he had his most beautiful smile on his face. I realized I have never noticed how beautiful his smile was. Until that evening.

He hugged me so strongly and said, "I missed you all day." Those words that he whispered into my ear, felt like electricity through my body. He and his energy were mashing with me and my energy so strongly and so deeply. I looked into his eyes, and sparkles of blue fell on me. *I should not be afraid of love anymore,* I thought.

I believed so much in him and I. In our perfect story. I trusted that he would understand my needs, that he would support my energy and talent, forever. And I was wrong. So wrong. I got fooled, I got trapped, *again*. Into lies, into darkness. It feels awful to lose hope again. I believed that it would be different this time. That I had found not only the prince, but a friend. Until I realized that he was seducing me with pretty words to take everything that I had. And then to leave me. I believed in him so much. I really thought that he understood and supported who I am.

Because I allowed myself to get off the healing train as soon as I got married, I stopped getting to know myself. Who am I and where do I want to go? It was easy for me to be whatever Adam told me I should be. And that was a kind, lovely wife who trusted her husband unconditionally. Even when people in her life try to tell her that she should look into what is really going on, and maybe that research assistant that is coming home so often is more than just an assistant.

But I didn't care. I wanted to believe that I did something right this time. Somewhere deep inside of me I knew that I would pay one day for my blindness. I was pushing through the days, one after another, allowing the distance to slowly grow between Adam and me. At the same time, his female colleagues and random new female friends were getting closer to him more than ever. Especially when I got pregnant, and I did not want to break up the family. And even more so when I lost the baby, *again*, and nothing seemed as important anymore.

* * *

If you are reading these lines,

Please know that you cannot wait for me.

I won't come to you anymore,

Not in this life that we know now.

Don't wait for me, my dear, you are losing time.

Don't wait for me, your life is passing by.

Please go your own way,

Find happiness where you once upon a time

Thought you would.

Don't wait for me, my sweetheart.

I cannot promise you a better life.

I can just give you some pieces from time to time,

Nothing more.

Go there, there, where you know what waits for you.

Be good.

Don't give yourself to me, my dearest.

Don't believe in this wine.

And when you find that happiness,

There, there,

Turn towards the East and smile.

I will know then that you are okay.

(Masha's journal entry)

* * *

Down beside the river,

I saw the shadow of you,

Waiting for me.

We did not know what destiny is bringing next for us.

But this was our thought-out goodbye.

I needed to see you,

To tell you how many lies crossed my mouth.

How many times I did not want to say how,

And what I truly felt for you.

Would I be brave enough to do that now?

To tell you how much I missed your lips,

Your laughter,

You.

While you were gone?

Will I be able to tell you the truth at least for goodbye?

Your hair was dancing on the wind,

I know you sensed me, that I am close to you.

I feel you will turn towards me soon.

Oh God! Am I strong enough to see her eyes again?

I am shaking like a leaf that if I do,

I will melt into her soul forever!

(Adam's poem written to Masha)

∗ ∗ ∗

I was gently waking up; the room was slightly lit by early sunlight. The bed was empty on the opposite side. The black silky sheets were untouched there. On my nightstand, electrolyte water was waiting and a post-it with a heart. I pressed the button above the lamp and the curtains started to open, letting the Sun completely in.

I tossed and turned a few times in the bed and then called Margaret in the kitchen. "Hi, Margaret. Good morning. How are you? Can you please bring me some coffee and water, and some breakfast? Thank you." I chose a loose, long dress for another hot day, some high-platform sandals, and my hair tied up in a bun.

Margaret was in the room already placing the breakfast on the balcony, where the Sun was beaming in. While I was doing my morning face routine, she was making the bed, and telling me the latest gossips about the new neighbours.

"Oh my God, they are like straight from a telenovela!" I said while laughing and Margaret promised more details in the next days.

My phone rang.

"It is Mr. Moore."

"Thank you, Margaret." I said while taking the phone. This morning, I was not so happy to talk with Adam. Not after the fight that we had last night at our friend's house.

"Yes?" I asked.

"Hi. How are you?" Adam's voice was breaking full of guilt, I hoped.

"I'm great. How about you?" I lied, and I knew he would not believe me. But what should I say? That I am falling apart yet again in my life, and that this is not the first nor the last fight that we will have. And that I promised myself that I wouldn't be in a bad marriage, that I do not want to lose years, energy, to give my soul and body again and again for nothing?

"I'm… okay. Do you want to have late lunch today with me?"

"Why not make it dinner then?" *I will be drunk enough by then*, I thought.

"Okay. Seven at Bocelli's."

"Okay." I hung up. In the meantime, Margaret left the room. I'm sure that she's heard many fights between Adam and me by now to know that she needs to retreat.

I went to the balcony and started with my coffee. Then I remembered my cigarettes; I started to smoke again. I pulled them from my bag and took that best first smoke with the first coffee. With the ocean view. Tears were melting my make-up. I ignored. I let it poor. Those were tears of despair and hope, love and betrayal, beginning and end. We are not placed in this life to know what will happen, even though we desperately try to figure that out. How was I supposed to know that Adam would hurt me, or maybe I made him hurt me? Life is given to us so that we live it the best way we can.

A few drops of my tears fell into my coffee. I left it back on the table. And continue enjoying my cigarette with an ocean view.

* * *

If I had known that such a beautiful, intense, and powerful love could turn into hate and destruction, I would most definitely choose to do a thing or two differently and not enter a relationship with Adam. I would practise self-control so that I never ever speak with him unless it is about work. And if I would ever sense that I am not strong enough anymore, I would change town, number, maybe even the country. I don't want to think that destiny would bring us together anyway, no matter where we are. But there, I thought that too. And even if that would happen, I would rationally, maturely, and responsibly choose to turn my head away. Literally.

Am I a person to ignore love? No, I am not. I go into love with open arms. So, yes, I would decide not to listen to my heart and rationally choose security over deception.

I fell for Adam so hard, so quickly, in the middle of my recovery from my previous loss. There was a hope, that he was just a bad cookie, and that it won't last. *Nothing that passionate and flammable lasts long.* That was one of my beliefs from my childhood. I was raised to believe that only the things that feel calm, easy, and stable, are the once that count. Everything else comes and goes and leaves us broken and alone. Since I worked so hard to change my old beliefs, to improve myself, I wanted to believe that Adam was something else, that he doesn't fit the mold. That he *was* my prince.

I remember the day when everything started to burn between us, the fire turning towards my soul, burning it completely. I remember the look in his eyes being distant and blurry, even though he was looking directly into my eyes and trying to be present. The semi-dark room, only the two of us, lots of petri dishes, the smell of ethanol, and a few tears of anger running down my face.

I was talking, trying to explain that he changed, that I feel it, that we need to work through things. I did not understand where this sudden change was coming from. And he, being angry and defensive, pointing out that there is no change whatsoever and that it is all in my head. Then I smelled the watermelon, and my intuitive mind rewound to the picture of the last month's Institute dinner, where he was serving watermelon to the newest member of the department. She was laughing pushing her small curls behind her ear, exposing her neck, while Adam was leaning towards her ear to tell her something. She was giggling, and he had the smile of a predator, feeding watermelon to his pray.

I buried that memory so deep. And now it came back so clearly! Anger that I have already felt, mixed with new waves of it, like a fire that started and will burn everything. Myself and everything around me.

"You better leave this room now." I said.

"Why would I? There are dozens of things to go through here, and you can't do this alone by tomorrow."

"So, I won't. And it won't be done, and then? You will lose money from the grant."

"Do you know how much I have worked on this grant? Don't you dare do this to me!"

"We are done here! Leave this room. *Now.*"

He took his backpack and slammed the door on the way out. I was standing in the same spot for I don't know how long. With tears of anger and disappointment coming down. I looked at all the work that was standing on the benches around me. I loved it, but I was not able to do anything, not at that moment. Also, there was no way to leave it all to go to waste, not because of Adam but because I wanted to know what the experiments would show. That is the only reason that I joined the project in Adam's laboratory. Because of science, not because of him. I wanted to do more experiments, besides the teaching, and we had a great idea on our minds.

I called Diana, another project lead, to help and cover as much as possible with her team. I told her that I didn't feel well and needed to remove myself from the lab. She generously said yes, and I thanked her for being such a sport. I packed my stuff and then I turned to my phone's texts.

Adam: *Don't forget to take the strawberries that I bought for you this morning at the market. They are on your shelf in the lab's kitchen fridge.*

In the middle of everything, me realizing the truth and our relationship breaking into pieces, he was still writing about some fruits that had to be eaten?

* * *

The warning signs were there for so long. Everything was lining up in my head now. I couldn't stay in the house, so I checked myself into a hotel. I needed to be alone, to think, to process. His eyes were so telling. There was no doubt anymore. I had flashes of situations from months ago; flirting with other women, which I at the time accounted to his charm; emails at the weirdest times, looks from some of his female students… This should not have happened! I already knew how this works. Mauricio taught me well how it feels to be cheated on. I should have known!

I was sitting on the hotel room floor, and I had no tears left. None. No compassion either. I had cried so much over men, that now I am dry as a desert. The anger subsided as well. I didn't have any negative feelings left to feel. There was only one thought in my head; *I am leaving Adam.*

If anything, through the years, I learned more than a little bit of self-respect. I love Adam and I don't want to condemn him for anything as I have yet to hear his side of the story, but I love myself more.

I will think of him; it will hurt. I need to remove all the hope and faith that I had in our marriage; it will make me suffer. I will need to change a big part of my life; it will be hard. But all of it will be necessary because this newer version of Masha loves herself. This Masha knows that she deserves a peaceful, loving life, where she feels safe and secured. *Finally.* And that is not with Adam. Not anymore.

The biggest truth was that I was here for the wrong reasons. I was in love with a mystery, with my imagination, with something that existed only in my head. He was just not into me. I fooled myself with the thought that he loves me, that he does everything for me, that he is my hero. Yes, he made me believe that too, it was not only me and my rose-tinted glasses. But I should have known that old lions do not change that easily. He was who he was, all his life. With his previous wife, with girlfriends. I foolishly thought that he changed, that he left his old life so that he can spend the rest of it with me. Because he smiled at me, he gave me hope. Or I believed he did, and he just had a smile on his face because it was the polite thing to do.

I will never know if any of it was true. And maybe it is better like that. Sometimes it is better to believe in anything then to know the truth. It hurts less. And when your life is filled with pain, being even more hurt by the truth, it hurts like hell. I thought, *maybe I am insane, maybe all the medications and therapy will never help.* If I am willing to change my whole life and the lives of people around me due to my own perception, and hurt everyone in the process, maybe it would be better if I find my life somewhere far away, from anyone that I have ever known.

* * *

I was walking on the beach, with my feet in the ocean. That was my way of releasing the energy when I needed to feel better. When I needed to not think to get in touch with my intuition. Believing in intuition was also another of those things that was making me 'less of a scientist.' It was not common for a scientist to believe in the unknown, not visible, not proven. I became happy that things started to change, even slowly. So, even though I was in California, I had to be careful how I used 'non-scientific terms' around certain people.

But I believed in intuition, and almost everything in my life was done with the help of it. I tried to listen to my gut feelings, or my dreams, or my visions, as I would listen to someone who has the best advice on the planet. And even if I made mistakes, according to critics of my life, I believe that no mistake is really a mistake but only a blessing, a lesson that had to be learned at the specific time.

While walking on the beach, a few days after I made my decision to leave Adam, I really needed to get in touch with my radical-self inside of me. I was in search of the best healing approach for my soul. I don't know how long I was strolling on the beach, up and down, until I realized that the Sun is setting on the horizon. And I did not get any information from my intuition. I sat on the sand and decided to watch the Sun disappear, going to sleep. Then something overwhelmed me suddenly. What if, after everything that happened in my life these years, all the trauma, tears, losses, I lost touch with my intuition? What if I cannot access it anymore? I was getting goosebumps thinking about it. It felt like I was an empty shell of the Masha I once was.

The sunset was beautiful, as many are from the west coast, looking over the Pacific, but my cheeks got wet for another reason. If I do not have my family and friends, at least not as close as they once were to me, if I do not have a love that I so desperately wanted to have, if my career is not fulfilling me, if I do not find reasons to smile anymore and if even my intuition left me, who am I? *What do I do now?*

It is funny though. When I realized that I did not see any positive thing in my life and that I had lost so much, I was still feeling only one thing that was coming out of me in the form of tears. I felt–peace.

What Needed
To Be Said

I believe in myself, but I believe more in You. You are
my Moon, my Sun, and my Cloud to sleep on.

It was painful to think that I will never see Adam again. The comforting thought was that he will be alive and well, but he will not be with me. He will not wake up in the morning by my side, and when I turn right, I won't see his messy morning hair.

I took my notebook and started to go through the pages of everything that I have written recently in it... And according to my records, I was not good about writing or noting my feelings... That is how it usually goes with me and my therapeutic poems. If my life is too busy and hectic, I just don't write. The last entry was last year, our vacation in Mexico. I think that was the last peaceful week we had before our separation. I closed my eyes and saw the beach, blue sky, us laughing, kissing, and drunk at four in the afternoon. Making love so gently those days, like never before, nor after. I felt the joy of him knowing how to kiss me, where to touch me, where to press harder. Several times a day. That was the week when we conceived Luna.

* * *

He was certain that he knows the right way to go.

He felt blue in her eyes,

And smelled green grass of home in her hair.

Everything that he ever loved and left behind,

Everything that he wanted and gave up,

In her smile, he could have seen.

"I love to know that I love to love you," he said.

He wanted to make new memories with her,

New lines in his book.

When all the pictures from the past

Where taken away from him that one day,

He wanted to find them,

Like Atlantis.

And now he was sure that he discovered

The way to travel into the past.

Because if we do not know the past, there is no future.

He hugged her black jacket at the crossroad,

That spring,

And all the senses got awaken.

It was impossible not to remember!

(Masha's journal entry)

* * *

"If someone does not want to be your friend, that is not your loss, that is their loss. They are not doing that *to* you, but *for* you. Trust yourself whole heartedly." These words were ringing in my head after meeting Luca for an emergency session.

Adam did not want to sign the divorce papers, nor did he show up to any of the mandatory meetings during the separation period. His lawyer was there, immaculately dressed of course, like any of his students from the rich families. I hated seeing her, I hated her instead of hating him. I hated her, with all my might, with all my unreasonable reasons. She represented everything that he placed between us, introduced into our marriage, like an entertainment, for him, his friends and all the people that wanted us to fail. I hated her red ponytail, and green eyes, and perfect red lips. I hated her precise sentences. Because deep down I wanted him to be present when all this, our life, is going down. I wanted him to see that I was not taking anything from him, that I just wanted out of the toxic relationship that ours had become. Seeing Adam again scared me, but maybe I wanted to see some guilt in him, finally. If he ever truly loved me. But he never showed up. Just his attractive lawyer to be a reminder of why this all was happening.

* * *

When the divorce came to an end, I was like–*oh no, this is the thing that I will never get over, another heartbreak, another disappointment.*

One night, I woke up in my own puke in the middle of the night. My stomach was so upset that it could not digest food. The realization came that I need to release my feelings, write them down. I wrote Adam an email.

Subject: At the end.

Hi Adam,

This is it, then... We are not watching the night sky together now. Our Universe does not exist anymore. I wish this pain that is in me is not so strong. Breathing is hard. I wish I could rationalize everything and move on, but I am not like that. I will never know the truth. I will never know your truth. I will never know what suddenly made you feel so uneasy with me. You wanted everything. You wanted something. You wanted nothing. You lied.

You tried to escape, and you wanted to stay. I will never know what was really going on inside of you. Remember the day when something clicked, and I guess we both had more desire to "fight" than discuss science? I think that was coming from all we kept inside: feelings, resentment, and hope that would never come out.

It does not matter how much time passes; my emotions towards you will always be there. So it is suitable for my health and life to say goodbye to the job too. It is hard to work at the same place as you. No matter how good I am at it and how much I will miss my students here, I must leave the Institute. In all our messy stories, we both learned that we are better with each other when we are not so close all the time.

I don't want to believe that I was wrong about everything. I still cannot accept that all the vows, all the poems, and all the laughter were just lies. And since I will never know the truth, I will believe my story. We loved. Then, one stopped to love the other. And we are now living separate lives. There are no kids to bind us. Luna did not want to come to us.

I am writing this email shamefully, and I have no other way but to trust that it goes to your heart only. And please do not respond to it. I would appreciate that very much. I count on your honest and gentlemanly side.

I still hope that one day I will see you on the street accidentally; I hope you will say hi. And we would have a chat about new lives. You would be happy, as would I.

Forgive me for everything that I did wrong to you.

I wish you all the best, to you and your future family,

Masha

Forgiving Myself

It was time to take an action. I needed a change. I spent months, *years* in therapy, talking, taking medications, working on myself. But now it was time to try to find my own path to feeling normal again. My normal. Smiling, dancing, breathing deeply. I did not want to feel like I would be crushed into the ground if someone asked me about my past.

The truth is that most of the time we have no idea what will happen with our lives. We want to believe that we do. That astrology or psychics would help us understand what the possibilities are; but in all honesty, we have no clue what our real future is. Most of the time we don't end up with the person that we thought we would. I could see my life so perfectly ready to be finalized with Adam, and then what happened? Life threw me a curveball, and Adam is no longer there.

And here is something more about conclusions and closures. For some time I did believe that I need to have that final, honest talk with someone to finish things in my heart. But that is such a disillusion. If I am sincere, every time that I wanted to see that specific person "for the last time,' I knew that it was just my hope that if we met once more, the person would realize that a mistake was made and that it is time to come back to me. So, no. Getting closure is just a prolongation of the inevitable. When it is over, it is over. For a reason. A reason that I don't always have to understand.

I did not get my closure with Francesco, and I never will. He is gone for a long time now. As is our unborn child. I just have a memory. He was taken away from me, or maybe I was never meant to be with him, and all of it was just a beautiful illusion. With no closure. The sight of the dead body of a loved one as an end. So, I do not believe in closure anymore. I do not need any with Adam. We were done that day when the papers were signed. And each of us did it alone, without the other. I did not need him to stand beside me and hold my pen while I sign. All the games were already played, and my heart has been already broken into pieces.

The hardest part is forgiving myself for all the men and wrong choices I have made, even those before Francesco and Adam. Even though I have no regrets, I felt judged, shamed, looked wrongly at, and that left a bitter taste in my mouth. I spent some sessions with a female therapist after Luca, to try to heal a bit, but nothing helped. So, I turned myself to faith.

I wanted to be a scientist who understands faith. Eventually, my soul brought me into a situation where I could achieve that. I moved to Greece, to a very small island, called Aegina. I knew enough Greek from my mother to have decent conversations with locals; I would improve while living among them. One day I was in front of this cute, small church, without knowing which religion it belonged to. Turned out to be a Serbian Orthodox church. It was morning and I heard singing from the inside. When someone opened the door to exit, I smelled sage, love, and kindness. I took a big breath and entered. No one was looking at me, no one was gossiping about me, no one knew me. It was an escape from the world that I was living in.

It seemed I found a bench filled only with a mother and her daughter. And I sat there and exchanged smiles with them. The liturgy was magnificent, and the priest talked about us, humans, not looking up enough into the sky, taking in all the hope that was so graciously given to us. Still, we are all looking only down into our phones and computers and judging other people for what they are and what they are doing. I cried that whole time while he was talking. For the first time, I felt like someone understands me.

* * *

Don't judge her

There she is, sitting on that stone.
She unravelled her long hair and used it to wipe her tears.
Sorrow is deep and black.
Sadness for all the dreams not dreamt yet.
For love which beginning was an end.
She should not have believed the wind,
There is no hope when thunder speaks soft words.
Only regret is left to bring pain in the chest.
Never spoken, forever buried.
If you ever love like her, you might understand.
But for now, do not judge her.
Let her sit alone and cry her soul out.
Everything that should not say to anyone.
Words to be forever underground.
Flesh tearing apart from the look.
Unpleasant burning behind left ear
From too many fake answers.
Every feeling must be burned.
Every move not made.
Maybe in the next life, if you still believe in that,
Maybe then souls find each other.

To hug and rest.

But now, do not judge her.

Let her sit and cry.

Let her wash herself with fake innocence.

It will pass soon.

There are just so many tears.

She will find some occasional comfort.

She will get up and put on the blue robe.

She will leave through the trees and rain, barefoot.

So that wounds remember.

She will go until that nowhere spot.

Where lions with wings are waiting.

But, for now, do not judge her.

(Masha's journal entry)

* * *

If you look into the darkness for a very long time, you forget that if you just turn your head into a different direction, you might actually see the light. It has been years since I last saw some brightness in my life. A dark blanket was covering me, and the light that I was searching for was impossible to see. Little by little, I was realizing that the light that I must find, or turn my head towards to, is not something that is outside. The light is inside of me. I am the light.

To be the light, you must allow yourself to be your true self, but not only in your own bubble, your comfort zone. Instead, you must be yourself anywhere, anytime. And that is the hardest part. It takes so much time to understand the fact that the light is inside of all of us, but to be fragile and open and expose your true self to others is an even longer, harder, more terrifying process.

All my life, I have known one type of Masha. Masha the people-pleaser, Masha who tries to understand everyone and help everyone, but deeply feels the pain of not being understood herself. Masha who postpones her healing for later because it doesn't fit in someone else's life plan at that moment. Masha who knew how guilty she felt for going to another country and living her life; leaving many people, including her mother, back in her home country, knowing that she misses them more than they miss her. Masha who even when she came back from Italy to her hometown, often felt ashamed and convicted for even the smallest things. The Masha that eventually burned out. And had a break down.

So, yes, it is an extremely long process for me to find who I am and light up the world with the 'true' Masha. To be honest, that process will never be completed. You do the work on yourself from the day you decide to feel better until the rest of your life.

The moment my light started to spark inside of me, I knew what had to be done next. I finally saw clearly what I wanted to do with my life. I found my inner animal. I was a Phoenix. I get reborn from the ashes of my past and my darkness, and my new life shines bright and warms me and anyone who enters my life. Suddenly, everything was in its perfect spot in my body, mind, and soul. The Phoenix spirit shines through!

* * *

I remember how once Luca was telling me that I should do an exercise where I would say or write myself a nice, compassionate letter. Where I would show that I can be warm and gentle with myself. Of course, back then, I did not do that. I did try, though. I was sitting for about an hour, and I surrendered the battle to my white screen. The concept of being compassionate towards myself was so distant to me. I knew we should be compassionate and gentle towards other people and help them when needed. But towards myself? Isn't it selfish? So, Luca told me to write a self-compassionate letter, like I am writing to my best friend when he or she is in need or in crisis. Even if it is short, like a message. Something that I could return to, read when I need it, or just do it and forget about it, to empty myself.

I did not do it when Luca told me, when I was back from Italy. But I was ready to try to do it after my move to Greece. I am not going to lie, it was so strange at first, but at the end of it… Oh boy, I felt much calmer. And I cried my eyes out. And I felt some peace.

Dear Masha,

I am so sorry that you are going through such a difficult time, I do not know how everything will turn out. For us. Because you are me and I am you… Gosh this is so strange! Right? Then I guess we both feel strange about this. And you know what? I think that is perfectly fine. We have every right to feel strange. To feel sad, depressed, to cry, to scream, to think that life is not fair. It has been enough of forcing ourselves to smile. Masha, you were so strong all those days after Franco died. You cried yourself to sleep and then you continued to go so fast through life again. Bravo, girl! You are awesome! But listen. Now you need to rest, now it is time to take really good care of yourself. Because life was not a comedy series! It was so hard. And you were fighting alone! You are the queen! Don't you ever forget how resilient you are and how much force and strength you have inside of you!

Who was there with you when all those men were hurting your soul? Who was wiping your tears all those nights when you were dealing with a crappy supervisor in Rome? Who was there when Franco died? Who was there when you found out that Adam cheated on you? And who was there when you shipped your boxes from the house and moved back to your family home, just so you can prepare for your move to Greece? And who is now with you when nights are colder and lonelier then ever?

You, Masha! Only you. You are your own stepping stone. You are the Moon that lights your road through the forest. You are your own best friend. And you know what? You passed all those difficult times, and you are still standing. Because you are stronger and more capable than you could ever imagine. And your life just started. There is a whole new future waiting for you to conquer! Except this time, you do not have to rush anywhere. Hurry slowly. Take it day by day. Find every day something to smile at, or to laugh about. Enjoy food, enjoy wine, enjoy walks, sleeping long and well. From now on, take care of yourself first. I will always love you!

Yours,

Masha.

* * *

I cannot fight any more for your attention.

So many others are around you.

I was only left to kiss your shadow and say goodbye.

I cannot compete for you, my love.

Either you love me or not.

Either you kiss me madly, or you turn your back to me.

You know, trouble is your middle name, and still,

I was always mad about every single detail about you.

So, you make love to me, or you do not.

I will not beg.

I take this last shot and leave.

You will have me, or you will lose me, forever.

It is up to you. Not me.

Do not blame me.

I am here.

Open.

Yours.

Honest.

You can have me, every inch of me.

If you are not afraid.

I am looking at you, my love.

And I want you, I do not hide.

I cannot hide it no more.

Take me.

Lose me.

I am waiting on your move.

(Masha's journal entry; the poem that she never gave Adam.)

My Time Will Come When I Rise Like A Phoenix

Maybe this is my time to be alone. Maybe I need this time to properly be with myself. I could never love you as much as I want to until I have Him under my skin.

She was sure that she knew the right way. She felt that in the blues of his eyes, and she smelled it in his hair, the green grass of her home. Everything that she loved, she left. Everything that she wanted; she gave up. But now everything is in his smile. "I love to love you," she said. She wanted to make new memories with him. New lines in her book. When all the memories from the past were taken from her, she wanted to find them, like Atlantis. And now, she was sure that she knew the right way for traveling into the past. Because if we do not know the past, there is no future. She hugged his black jacket at the train station that spring and all the emotions woke up. It was impossible not to remember.

I was sitting one Sunday noon in a tavern called *Aleksandar*. Greek folk music was playing, and that place served the best coffee. I lit my cigarette and let out a circle of smoke towards the sky.

I was thinking about Adam, Francesco, and Mauricio. All three of them carved such a paramount line in my life. Each one of them in their own way. I would never be who I am now without my experiences with each of them.

The passion and the craziness of Mauricio's spirit, in my twenties. He did love me in his own way, and he tried to be beside me when terrible things happened in my life. He taught me what a fancy restaurant was like, and which are the good clubs. He showed me good music and taught me science. But there was also a lot of abuse and misuse, a lot of lies, a lot of tears. Because I let him, I didn't know better. Because I loved him the best I could for my first serious boyfriend, whom I wanted to marry.

And now we are here, across the globe, at a small island, which my ancestors once called home. We are here, spirits of all the people I have known and myself, my angel, my prayer, and my salvation. Sometimes, you must spend years of your life in anger and roar to come to the peaceful stream. You didn't lose while you waited. Sometimes you need a little bit more hope and warm-heartedness than any other action. I trust and hope, *again*, that this is the end of a long search. Following my heart and my true self, I am allowed to be consumed by the belief that I am at the place where I should be.

While the day was passing by, I was remembering what Luca was telling me. That the most important lesson that I need to learn is to really love myself. With that, no matter who treats me in which way, I will have myself to return to. I will have me.

So maybe it is my destiny to be alone, and not have a lover by my side. Maybe it is okay that I don't have my own kids, I can be a mother to any kid that comes to this village. Maybe my soul talks to my predecessors and knows that this is the best way for me, without too much thinking and analysing.

✶ ✶ ✶

The next day, I visited the monastery adjacent to the Serbian orthodox church I visited upon my arrival. The bishop was praying, so I stayed at the door to avoid disturbing him.

"Come my child, come," he called to me, eyes closed, not even turning to see who it is.

"I did not want to interrupt you; I am so sorry."

"Why do you think you are? No, I was just praying for you. For your health and faith."

"Me?" I felt honoured, but, *why me?*

"Yes, I feel that you are getting settled here, but also, settling too much is not good for a woman like you. You still need a family; you need faith that someone will deserve you."

He showed me to sit on the chair beside the candle store, and he sat on the other beside me.

"You suffered a lot my child. You are full of heaviness inside of you. And you are carrying that with you like it is something to be proud of. Like you need to be sad, to prove something to the world."

Tears started to fall down my cheeks. He was right. But how can I be happy again?

"Those people who really loved you, they would want you to love again. And be happy. Because that is love."

* * *

The day before my visit to the monastery, I received a letter from Adam. I was a bit scared to open it. I did not know what to expect from him at this point. I did not take anything from him; it was cutting the cord, painful, but clean. Also, how did he know where to send the letter? Sophie, *Sophie...* So, I did not open it. Not that day. I placed it in the drawer with my jeans and I forgot about it. Until the priest mentioned people who once loved me.

I was praying that when I open the drawer, the letter won't be there, but when I placed my hand under the pile of jeans, I felt it. *It is real.* I pulled it out and placed it in my handbag. And I went to the beach to find a spot to read it.

First, I placed it on my heart, closed my eyes and prayed that he listened to the saying, "if you don't have anything nice to say, don't say anything." Second, I opened it and started to read.

Hola Masha,

I wanted to write, 'mi amor,' but I guess that would not be appropriate. If you are wondering, yes, Sophie gave me the address. You really went far away. Is it from me? Or is it the big life change? Are you staying there permanently? I guess what I am trying to say, I miss you here. LA is not the same without you. The campus is not the same without you. There was a joy you were bringing here, and now it is gone. I probably should not write this either, but I am.

All my life I was waiting for someone like you. The first time I saw you, I knew it. You were the girl! You were the one, after searching and trying and failing. I honestly haven't seen the end of us. Ever. And I blew it. It is my fault. Because you were there, you were everything that anyone can want. You ARE everything that I want. Still. There, I said it. I lost the most precious jewel that I have ever had. Because I know that you won't come back to me, I saw resentment in your eyes. That won't go away, I know you. And I am destined to be without you. To lose you. To see you leave me.

I am sorry. That is all I can say. I can tell you that if you would give me another chance, I would not repeat the same mistake, but I cannot ask that from you. You loved me truly, you healed for me. And I broke that heart again. I deserve your resentment and hate.

I am really sorry. If you ever find it in your heart to forgive me, you would mend me. This broken soul has no right to ask you anything. But if you ever find the space in your heart, to forgive me, send the energy this way.

I miss you, Masha.

We will never see tomorrow, but I will always see you in my mind, the first thing when I wake up and the last thing before I go to bed.

I will always love you. That might explain why I was not present for all the paperwork, or mediations, or the final signing. I couldn't watch how we are falling apart.

And you, you deserve to find someone who will not break your heart again. You deserve a man that I wish I was for you. And I hope one day I will hear that you did find one. You deserve love until infinity and back! You are the best woman I have ever met.

With love,

Adam

P.S. I have found this picture of us from the first benefit dinner we went to together. Look at us. SO happy! And so, in love. If I just hadn't let it slip away.

* * *

Boundaries were never something that I was good at. When I started to work with Luca years ago, we came to the realization that I had none. I was giving myself to others even if they did not ask me to. Saying 'no' was a non-existing action in my life. Everything that I did or said was with the idea of 'I want other people to like me, love me. I want to be loved, and if I want to achieve that, I need to behave as other people want me to'. That is why I needed to start making boundaries, even if they are extreme.

Going to Rome to continue my career as a scientist was not solely decided because of the possibilities that would await me there; as much as it sounds unbelievable–who wouldn't want to go to Rome to live there and fall in love as I did! That sounds like something that had been done with the full free will, but it wasn't. Falling in love in Rome was a massive reward, as well as a massive pain, but was not in my plans…

I went to Rome to escape. From the chaos of my family, from the tears and sorrows that I had with Mauricio, from my life. I felt forced to leave, while I really didn't want to. I needed my family, I wanted to work on our relationships, but when my mother showed that she is not interested in deeper conversations with me, something inside of me died. The distance between us was present even before I left. So, when she commented that, *'yes, you should go abroad and explore'*, I left. That night, before I left LA, I was crying myself to sleep. My adult self was utterly overwhelmed by my hurt young self.

* * *

I decided to write a letter to Adam.

That decision was on my mind for quite some time. However I didn't do anything about it immediately. I did not have the will to type or to take a pen and paper. But one relatively chilly, late September evening in Greece, I felt that it is the perfect time to do so. I had it in me. I reached the stage of acceptance, finally. And I needed to seal it. Seal with my words. Pen and paper. A cup of tea. Candles. The smell of the salt in the air.

Hi Adam,

It took me awhile to get my words in order and in line with my emotions, so that I can sit and write you this letter.

Gosh, even today it feels like you are everywhere! I have moments where I just want to call you and tell you how my day was and what were my highlights. I know that over time it will get better, but now, I still miss you. Jesus, I loved you! I loved you so much!

And I guess I will always love you in some way. For now, I am allowing myself to be aware of my emotions. Because I know that if I bury them deep inside of me, I will never be able to move on. And I do not mean to move on as 'I have another man'. No. I need to move on for me. I need to clean my energy; I need to remove and cleanse all the stale and old from my soul. I need to be alive and awake again.

It took me a lot of time to come to this stage, where I can accept that we are over. I could not hate you at first, but when it came to me, the emotions of anger and hate were so intertwined and strong. Oh my God, I thought it would never be over! Because I was finally realising: You were lying to me. You were lying. You lied about everything. And I was so certain that I would vanish every memory that I have about us! That I will not allow myself to remember you or us!

But then I would hear a song that brings flashes of light from back then… When we were. Oh, I wish so much to hate you forever. But I can't. Because when that specific smell is in the air, there are those glimpses of us again. All of it comes back… Those nights, the laughter, the promises. And I realize that I still love you. And that I always will. Because I forgave you for all of it. I won't forget, but I forgave.

So, instead of sending you negative vibrations, when I think of you, I will send you love and peace. May you be loved. May you be at peace. And may I be free.

Lots of love,

Masha.

* * *

I remember the last time I've seen Adam. He was meeting me in the campus park to bring me my favorite book, which I had forgotten. It was hiding in the sheets, and I didn't notice it while packing. I could have bought another copy, and the meeting was unnecessary, but both of us needed that moment.

When I saw him from a distance, I was shocked by all the emotions that went through my body. First, I felt like I was seeing him for the first time. There was a feeling of joy that he was heading in my direction. I was blushing like a schoolgirl! Then, I saw that he saw me too, and he became more aware of his steps, which made him seem like he actually cared how he will look like to me. I felt love. Because I loved Adam, I love Adam, and despite all odds, I will always love him.

When he was just a few feet away from me, he stopped, looked directly into my eyes and said, "Hi, Masha."

"Hi, Adam," I said with every little bit of strength that I had in me to keep the eye contact and look like I am not upset, I am not sad, I am a human being with no emotions. But I was never good at lying to him, so I guess he could see how I was burning from inside out, and how desperately I wanted to kiss him at that moment, no matter the pain.

He reached his hand towards me and handed me the book. Then the eye contact stopped. We were both standing in our own spot, looking at the ground. No words. No courage to say anything else. I do not know how long that moment lasted, but when the air between us was so thick that we could not breathe anymore, we both looked at each other again. He came at me quickly, hugged me and said, "Take care, Masha."

I was silent until he turned his back and started to walk away. "You too. You too, Adam."

I do not know if he heard me. And there they were, my first tears that meant–I lost him. We are really giving up on us. I do not know why that was still in me, that hope that he maybe will never give up on us, that he would fight for me, I do not know. But apparently it was there. I became aware of that.

However, Adam was not that type of prince…

* * *

It was so easy to decide to be bitter and resentful, but somehow my soul could not cope with that. Truthfully speaking, in the beginning of my newly-divorced life, I did take some of that bitch-from-the-dark attitude, and I kind of liked it. I would dress as I wanted, drink as much as I wanted. 'Flirting and then rejecting' was my favorite part of my game. And at times, I did not feel any guilt for the men that were experiencing my outbursts. I have been through enough! And I decided that I had every right to be whoever I wanted to be. So I took a role of 'you will regret that you want me' type of a woman. And it felt so good!

It took work and action to remove some pain away from my soul so that my intuition awakens and slowly shows up in the small signals every day. That same intuition stopped me on my way to becoming a bitter lady that will singe you with her words if you come try to interact with her.

When I returned to my 'normal' state, where I find pleasure in being in comfortable pyjamas and watching the same cheesy movie with a tear or two, I did feel bad about placing so much bad energy towards men that crossed my path recently. They were not Mauricio, nor Adam. They might not leave me like Francesco did, and they did not deserve to be punished by my fears. Anyway, what is done is done and I can only have faith that I will be forgiven for those actions.

One evening, some days before the decision to go to Greece, I finally felt I wanted to keep my hope that one day things will get better. I wasn't thinking about finding a new husband not even a boyfriend. I was hoping to find my new, better version of me. I wanted to collect all the pieces that were broken, and rebuild, renovate, rise from the ashes as the new Masha. Stronger, gentler, more loving and carrying for herself and others.

And I was looking forward to that amazing road that was in front of me!

* * *

It has been a year already since I have arrived in Greece. Days were easy, predictable, slow paced. I loved it! I am waking up with a smile on my face, greeted by the blue sky and Sun's warm rays, while birds and the sea are singing my wake-up song. My empathy and intuition are finally awake, and I am enjoying every moment of it.

Since I started to help in the local Serbian monastery and adjacent church, I have learned so much about the religion itself, all the customs that people follow. Not that long ago, I converted to the Serbian orthodox religion. I feel so much more connected with the people and their suffering, and I try to help in any way I can. From a few lessons from the local healer, I now know how to heal simple things, such as wounds, fever, and coughing, and I invest my energy into helping people think more positively. Scientifically, I know how that impacts the brain and the mind, and I am doing this in real-time with real people who need help and with myself, too, since my healing is far from being done.

Life is not simple, life is not easy, many times in my life I have been shown that. And there is no Prince Charming that will come to help you. You are your own Prince Charming. Even if it looks like someone just appeared in your life, just like that, poof, it is not an actual surprise. You were praying hard for that; you made some decisions you might have forgotten. But you made some steps; you did it! And then, miracles happened.

Another thing that I am currently learning is–life is magic. We were created by a magical touch of our Creator. From the beginning of time, people were witnessing miracles being performed. And there will be more of them, until the end of time.

I am witnessing miracles now every day. A child's smile, a grateful look from the woman that had a bit of pain relief after I applied some medicine. And I am soaking up all of that, breathing in all that gratitude and love. The country is not rich or filled with yachts and fancy houses; but it is the wealthiest country that I have seen. Wealth is in the positivity, ability to change the perspective and have a different view on the situation. People here are growing their own food, making their wine, and have a longer lifespan than other countries in Europe. They are believers, and faith is an integral part of their life.

But what I enjoy the most are those clear-sky nights when people gather, sometimes it feels like the whole village is there, with so many stars that are covering us with a blanket of awe and hope. Some of the people are then singing traditional songs from their region, sharing food and drinks. Connection and love are what is important here. And I feel blessed every time when the chills of satisfaction spread all over my body. What else would one want in their life?

* * *

You can never really know how your life will end up. You can hire astrologists, chakra readers, energy healers, you can use tarot cards, crystals; just about anything, but you will not know how your life will turn out.

I was convinced that I was going to be a scientist, who works in a laboratory every day, happy, experimenting, having freedom and fun with science, who also teaches and loves it! But many years in academia taught me that being a woman, without a help of an older, "wiser" man, preferably a scientist as well, gets you nowhere. Feeling like an imposter after studying for 20 years is just one of the things that you go through. There are those situations where, as a woman in science, you are supposed to dress and behave a certain way. You need to fit the mold. And I was far from a person who would fit the mold. I did not *want* to fit the mold, ever. I wanted to be me, as unique as possible. That was not liked by my colleagues.

Academia taught me that injustice is a real thing. And yes, maybe because of Adam, I believed for a second that I will stay in the system, but that split second was over fast. As fast as our marriage. I could not stay in academia after the divorce. That was just not possible. I was not looked at as 'Masha, PhD'. I was now 'Masha, Adam's ex and PhD'.

Nostradamus himself could not predict the depth of the emotional crisis that I had in my life. The disrupted family. The career turnabouts. The turmoil of one hard relationship after the other. And yet, here I am, alive, breathing, feeling thankful for every day of my life.

* * *

Maybe my country is Greece. Maybe my therapist is a Serbian orthodox priest in Aegina. Maybe my medication is the tastiest wine I have ever had. And maybe I meet my perfect man here. Or not. My life goal is to rise again like a phoenix from the ashes of my life; new, strong, and limitless.

Epilogue

Born in the year of many world distortions. In the Month of the Moon of Balance. In the Night of the Full Moon in Pieces. Born to live and breathe the opposites. The synergy of reason and emotion. To always be on the edge of total disaster. I remember one of my astrology sessions. The astrologer told me that I was born to be polarized and to always be pulled between two sides. That I would be always overly emotional but make decisions that are practical. And ultimately never be completely happy. Unless I learn how to manage both and live in balance. Unless I find peace in knowing that life is not fair and that this world is broken, but that there are things that I could deeply love and give myself entirely to. I am living that truth, right now.

* * *

I had a dream.

You were coming from the shadows,

Surrounded by the red light.

I was not afraid.

Your eyes were looking at me, telling me,

That You care.

So, I believed.

I allowed you to take me into Your light,

To become one with You.

I could feel like I am safe and at peace.

You whispered into my ear,

That You were waiting for me.

I touched Your hand to acknowledge,

How long I waited for You.

I was told not to trust creatures from the shadow,

But I trust You.

With my soul.

I am signing the contract that You gave me.

Now I am Yours.

You are my Saviour.

You are my Reason.

You hug me with Your wings,

And we are transitioning to the place of Love.

I had the dream.
Of You and I.
Now, I am living in a constant search,
For the Creature with the Red Wings of Light.
I am living for finding You. Again.

(Masha's journal entry; one year upon arrival to Greece)

Acknowledgements

I would like to express my sincere and heartfelt appreciation to Keidi Keating and her publishing house, Your Book Angel, whose role as both editor and publisher has been invaluable to the creation of this novel. Her expertise, support, dedication, and belief in this project have completed it. With that help, my dream of publishing a book manifested.

My deepest gratitude goes to my father, Tugomir, mother, Ivanka, and sister, Maja. They will always be the never-ending source of energy and light for everything I do. They have been a constant wellspring of inspiration throughout the writing process.

I would also like to extend a special, loving thank you to my husband, Sascha, whose unconditional support and belief in me have been a massive source of strength and motivation. Thank you for reading my first draft and being patient with my articles. Thank you for accepting who I am and supporting me to openly be what I want to be.

Lastly, I am grateful for the myriads of life lessons and experiences that have gave this novel's foundation. Each life experience has provided me with invaluable insights and inspired me to shape the stories and the characters that you can find within the pages of this book. To all who have been part of my life and gave me exactly what I needed at the given moment, I offer my truthful thank you.

About the Author

Selena Đorđević-Marquardt was born and raised in Pirot, Serbia. She is a scientist by vocation, with a Diploma in Molecular Biology and Physiology and a PhD in Biochemistry. More importantly, she is a dreamer and a lightworker. This is her first novel. She currently lives in La Jolla, California.